WIFE SWAP

THE HOPELESS HUSBAND SERIES

AHAVA TRIVEDI

Wife Swap: The Hopeless Husband Series

First published, January 29th 2019

Formatted by Drew A. Avera.

To my mum, Shashi.
You've always been there for me no matter where I am and what I do.
Your heart is boundless and I've learnt most from you since I became a mum
– I'm so lucky to have you as mine.

CHAPTER ONE

The tiny staffroom was abuzz with the Monday morning meeting that had been called by Mr. Flounders, Summerfield Community School's headmaster. Normally, these meetings were left to deputy heads or those with far less seniority but not on this occasion. Teachers were teamed up in small groups, typically with colleagues from the same department, murmuring in anticipation about the cause for the head's sudden appearance.

The consensus amongst a few heads of department, snuggled in the middle of the room was that perhaps, Mr. Flounders had decided to resign or take an abrupt sabbatical since a couple of big grants for the school had recently fallen through. The headmaster didn't take set-backs well. He was especially ill-equipped at handling ones that entailed a loss of funding for the school, which he dreamed would one day be the most pristine in the whole country.

Jody Cresswell, the school's walking tabloid newspaper, had placed herself as far away as possible from the geeks that taught in the mathematics department – her own discipline. While to students and parents she often used her subject as an easy way to carve herself out as the intellectual cream of the teaching profession, in the company of her peers she openly shunned the stereotype they represented. She periodically shook her head, causing her golden corkscrew curls to lap up and down as she gave animated revelations about what she'd learned about one of the drama teachers in the line at canteen last week. Her cronies consisted of a multidisciplinary gaggle of gossip-mongers that soaked up the information eagerly, as though it held the hidden power to bestow them with bouts of joy that their own lives were by comparison, slightly better than the plight of their victim.

"Poor Eva Batchford, as if it isn't bad enough that she's stuck prancing around, teaching a bunch of prickly teenagers how to act. Now her husband has only managed to run them into over ten-thousand pounds of gambling debt behind her back! It's just too wretched to comprehend!" Jody conveyed, as her colleagues nodded dementedly. She carried on disclosing or perhaps fabricating, some particularly juicy details.

"Some birds really know how to pick a bloke," agreed Darren Easy, a capricious physical education teacher who had benefitted on numerous occasions from the lapsed judgement of women.

"Of course, I'd never stand for anything of the sort in my marriage. Michael and I have always maintained openness and honesty since we were first dating. It's the only way." Jody shook her head again as a couple of the women in the group agreed, gazing at her in admiration.

Emma Blue, who taught music at the school and had no idea how she'd ended up in the midst of Jody and her crowd, shuddered at the mindless drivel she'd been inadvertently subjected to. She moved quickly, taking a step backwards to put some palpable space between herself and the group.

"And God only knows what music teachers' lives must look like on the inside," Jody hit back in response to noticing that she was the object of Emma's repulsion.

"They look the same as everyone else's – perfectly fine until you have the need to make up pointless and vicious rumours about them," Emma smiled sternly, maintaining her distance. She tucked a stray strand from her otherwise perfect, silver bob behind her ear and skimmed the room for friendlier faces.

John and Franny Webb both walked in, though not together. There was an air of discontent between the two of them that Emma spotted the moment she saw them walk through the set of heavy wooden doors.

Franny appeared like she was ready for the warmth of summer in a soft blue, cotton dress. It perfectly matched her brunette waves, complete with her naturally frosty highlights. Though her face had the same ever-approachable warmth to it and bore no trace of disgruntlement, Emma knew something was bothering her friend behind that gentle demeanour. Her husband was the dead giveaway. He was even more dishevelled than he normally was. The only blazer he owned, which consisted of a worn tweed fabric with shabby leather patches sewn in at the elbows, was done up lopsidedly, with one end higher than the other. The faded wisps of hair that framed his forehead were tousled as though he'd ventured through a forest in the grip of a powerful hurricane. His garish red tie with a mess of indiscernible shapes printed all over it was slung limply over his left shoulder as if it too, had succumbed to the same forces that its owner had found himself at the mercy of.

"Morning!" Emma greeted Franny, as John Webb disappeared through a space of bodies, heading straight for the kettle in the corner of the room.

"Hi there!" Franny smiled, looking happy for the change in company.

"How's everything?" asked Emma as the two of them made their way straight to the line-up for the kettle, cups in hand.

"Oh good, how about you?"

"Good, good. Charlie and I, well mainly I, decided that we'd like to get our kitchen renovated so we were just window shopping all weekend. B&Q had a few interesting options but really, I'd like to go for something a little more avant-garde so I ended up dragging poor Charlie around to a few places," said Emma, feeling eased from her encounter with Jody.

"That sounds like a productive weekend," said Franny, dimming a little and then immediately brightening up as she was never one to rain on someone else's parade.

"Yes, we'll get there with something that's right for us, eventually. How was your weekend?"

"You, know – the usual." Franny stared inside her yet-to-be-filled coffee cup, hoping to conjure up some equally noteworthy details about her own weekend. When she couldn't find any, she gazed back at Emma, wondering what else she might have been up to. They shifted to the front of the line and Franny took hold of the kettle and peeped inside to check the water level.

"I couldn't help but notice that you and John...is everything well with you both?" Emma asked watching the tea-bag in her cup start to buoy up and down as Franny poured steaming water over it. She proceeded to add to her own cup, instantly wafting the aroma of freshly brewed coffee.

"Err, yes, you know us. We're as boring as a pair of brown socks compared to you and Charlie."

"That's not true! Not in the least. I'd say John really upped his game a couple of months ago on your anniversary – even if he did get there in his own weird – and wonderful – way."

"Please don't remind me..." groaned Franny, rubbing one of her temples like she had just remembered she had a terrible headache.

"The dinner was fine, don't feel bad about that – if anything it's given us all a good story to share and laugh about for years to come.

"Charlie found it enthralling that John went so out of his way to do his big debut with dinner, even if he did end up trying to pull off a pizza from Pizza Hut as his own!"

"It's not that, Emma. Actually, it's funny you mention that awful occasion – this morning changed everything."

"I thought you'd both been getting along like two love birds since that evening?" Emma was confused.

"I wouldn't go that far but yes, things had been considerably better until it hit me that the positive changes were more in my mind than in my marriage." Franny seemed stricken.

"What happened?" enquired Emma with unfurling curiosity.

"Do you remember how he gifted the two of us with a trip to Paris?"

"Of course! That was the part that was so wonderous – you'd wanted to visit Paris with him for twenty-five years. What a perfect anniversary present to finally wake up and come through on it!"

"Unfortunately, Emma, all wasn't what it seemed on that score."

"What the devil do you mean?" asked Emma.

"I brought up Paris at breakfast this morning. I thought that John was just being coy or more possibly, lazy, on those other occasions when I've raised the details of the trip, like setting a date and the like. Today when I brought it up, he pretended to choke on a piece of sausage and I knew there was more to it."

"And was there?"

"You can bet there was. I pushed him to tell me what was going on and he finally gave in and showed me the plane tickets."

"And?" asked Emma, dying to know how and where it was possible to go wrong in such a seemingly simple situation.

"He never booked Paris. The restaurant he booked for us is in the Czech Republic. And the plane tickets are to Prague."

"Why?" Emma understood less than she had a minute ago.

"Because he's obsessed with Franz Kafka," moaned Franny.

"Who's that?"

"He was a Czech author from Prague. So of course, my present is one that caters solely to John's interests." Franny was forlorn.

"I'm speechless. I'm sorry – and knowing how much you love Paris and have wanted to go there for so long. If it helps, I'd be livid if I were you."

"That's because if Charlie did something like that, it would be totally unlike him. Your anger would be justified because such a selfish act would catch you off guard."

"Yes but –"

"I should have known better. This is exactly what John

does. He thinks I'm cross with him but if anything, I'm cross with myself for building things up and allowing myself to expect something so out of the bounds of his capability that I was asking the impossible."

"But Franny, everyone deserves to feel wanted in their relationship. John's behaviour only serves him." Emma could feel her own indignity rising like a snake that was being charmed by frustration.

"And I knew what he was like when I married him. Why I thought he'd change, I haven't the slightest clue."

"What are you going to do?" asked Emma, thoughtfully.

Franny was just about to answer when Mr. Flounders entered the crowded staffroom with his troupe of deputy heads. They marched over to the only window in the dingy space and assembled themselves in a line, like a class of students waiting to be picked for a football team. The head-teacher was strategically in the middle, folding and unfolding a few leaves of crumpled paper as he waited for everyone to quieten down. His black hair was so slick with styling gel that it stiffly reflected back glints of the sterile white lighting from above. It was just before the morning tutorial and the smell of mixed grounds made the place smell more like a coffee shop at a train station than a staffroom. Mr. Flounders cleared his throat arbitrarily to silence a few teachers at the other end of the room, who still hadn't finished their nattering.

"Morning everyone," he began. "I thought I'd use this opportunity to announce an innovative new way we're going to raise funds for Summerfield."

Many teachers appeared relieved, having been anxious about much larger changes. Some tuned in with interest and others quickly zoned out. Franny eyed John Webb across the room and as expected, confirmed by his signature expression of a glazed cherry, the old man was miles away from the meeting at hand. Of course, she thought. Upon questioning, her husband would have blamed Mr. Flounders for not specifying that mental presence was as necessary as physical attendance, sooner than taking responsibility for his own minute concentration span.

Gazing further afield, Franny also saw that Darren Easy and most of Jody Cresswell's group had followed suit with her husband but acceptance for other colleagues spacing out came much easier and didn't prove wildly irritating the way John Webb's behaviour did.

"As you've all probably heard, the school has lost a lot of money recently. Some of it was due to unfortunate events beyond our making where the organization backing us fell into difficulty with its financial books.

"And also because of events closer to home." Mr Flounders involuntarily aimed a frown in John Webb's direction. He recalled that fateful assembly where the old man's actions had dashed his hopes of an art grant that had been in the bag.

John Webb was so zoned out that he was the only one who failed to register the headteacher's derision. Franny instinctively felt responsible for her husband's actions, foxed as to how he could continue to be so blissfully ignorant amidst the blatant tension. Emma watched Franny shudder as she thought back on the assembly where John Webb had turned himself into a spectacle when his German class had read out love letters to Franny, that he'd tried to secretly pass off as his own.

"It was truly awful, what happened that day in front of that gentleman from The Arts Council," tutted Jody, shaking her head and throwing her ample curls into motion once more.

"Yes. But we at Summerfield are about moving forward in the most innovative ways possible," said Mr. Flounders, looking around and then down at his papers. Jody Cresswell nodded vigorously. If she felt snubbed, she hid it well.

"It is my pleasure to announce that my senior team and I have brainstormed the most unique approach, maybe in the whole of Great Britain, to bring attention to the school and to raise its profile." Mr Flounders folded his papers and placed them on a nearby table.

"Sounds amazing," remarked Darren Easy, pretentiously.

"The plan can be solid but it's the people that make it outstanding," said Mr. Flounders. "And in this case, I look to some notable members of our staff right here, in this room, to help bring the vision to light."

"We'd love to do anything we can to help," Jody tried again, hitting the mark.

"I'm delighted to hear it!" Emma detected the slightest note of anxiety, as the headteacher, reached over and retrieved his sizeable pile of papers from the desk. He cleared his throat. "Starting today, those of you who are married or in a live-in relationship will be part of a sponsored wife swap. It's all been arranged, you'll be going home after school to pack your things tonight, as you shall be moving in with your new spouse."

CHAPTER TWO

Most of the staffroom jolted into wakefulness. Hushed, yet audible voices began to chatter bemused at what Mr. Flounders had just said. The deputy heads worked the crowd with smiles menacingly pasted on their showy faces. The headteacher gazed around, as though he'd just bestowed a generous surprise bonus out of his own pocket and was waiting for the staff to let it sink in before thanking him. When no one commented and he noticed some teachers standing near him even began staring at their feet or got out their phones in open avoidance, he continued.

And for this carefully crafted effort, we're getting our very own segment on national television – the BBC is interested in showcasing the school through your stories!"

Mr. Flounders paused to let everyone absorb what he believed to be exalting news but if he expected applause, it didn't come. Instead, a quiet chatter rose up once more, amongst the groups standing before him.

"A wife swap? Good Lord, sounds a bit sexist, doesn't it?" whispered Emma, so only Franny could hear.

"In my two decades plus at Summerfield, I've never

heard anything like it," said Franny, louder than Emma. A handful of teachers in the vicinity nodded at her summation.

"Very funny, is this one of those bits where you get us to believe something really ridiculous and the moment we're on board, you tell us what we'll really be doing?" asked Eva Batchford, a petite woman with delicate elfin features who immediately turned a shade comparable with her fiery red, pixie-cut hair. She tentatively poked her head out from behind a huddle of drama teachers, who'd been acting as a human shield for her from Jody's onslaught. Her immense eyes, dazzling like a pair of robin's eggs, searched for a trace of humour in Mr. Flounder's expression, before she self-consciously receded back into anonymity.

Franny and Emma both knew Eva Batchford as skittish and meek at the best of times. The three had been working closely together, on a production of *Grease* since the past couple of months and in exactly two weeks, the show would be performed live in front of what would hopefully turn out to be a packed hall. Emma was helping with musical arrangements and singing and Franny had offered to use her after-school art class on Thursdays as a venue to create some of the backdrop and props for the musical. It had been a thoroughly enjoyable effort so far and it was always a pleasure when students became immersed in something that sparked the flicker of creativity within. However, anytime that the two friends had approached Eva with a gesture of friendship, she'd treated them with unwarranted suspicion. Franny assumed the trust issues to be due to the torrents of gossip about Eva's personal life and she begrudgingly indulged in thinking that *if* what Jody had been saying had some truth to it, the poor woman had enough to deal with at home.

"Come on everyone, I'm not joking," said Mr. Flounders, trying to be playful but still convey seriousness.

"He's not. It's actually a stroke of genius," agreed Natalie Stone, a sallow looking woman, the only female deputy head at the school.

"We wanted to come up with something that reflected our headteacher's flair and what better than his favourite show?"

"Cheeky perv," said Darren Easy, winking and offering Mr. Flounders a remote high-five.

"Some of you will be the ambassadors of our fundraising efforts by taking part in a wife swap. It's all voluntary of course but the senior team has practically done the work for you." Mr. Flounders ignored the remark and smiled through the rising air of tension.

"Can we have some more details?" asked Ludwig Suneyes, a keen, young teacher who'd joined the Modern Foreign Languages department only a couple of years ago. John Webb who was leaning against a wall right next to where Ludwig was, startled awake as he spoke.

Ludwig Suneyes wore a serious expression, ever ready to either issue or take instructions. His cropped hair and love of discipline had swiftly led Jody Cresswell to speculate that the young man must have had a stint in the British military before becoming a school teacher. She'd thought it worth speculating that Ludwig's former career must surely have ended abruptly after being shamefully sacked by the Ministry of Defence. Obviously, she'd conveyed her misinformation to anyone within earshot before the teacher had even finished his first week at the school.

"Of course, I'm so glad there's interest!" Mr. Flounders began handing the papers around the room. "Now, I could just call out the names of those of you who will be participating, with your permission of course, but I don't want to sound like we're in a classroom with our students.

"Instead, as I pass these around, take a look and if you see your name, keep the paper but if you don't, just pass it along. Even if you aren't on the list, I encourage you to stay for the details so that we can all support each other as a team."

Emma Blue read down the list as she eyed the paper that had been passed to her and instantly spotted both hers and Franny's names on one sheet.

"I don't see any of *their* names on here," she said through gritted teeth in reference to the school's senior management.

"Were we lucky enough to be swapped with each other?" asked Franny recognizing as soon as she said it, that if that were the case, the luck would have been solely hers.

"They've really turned it into a sideshow. Look, there's a number next to each name. All the women are separated out from the men and we have to look on another sheet to find our match," Emma shook her head.

The other papers eventually made their way around and as Franny and Emma began skimming through, Jody Cresswell mowed her way through the crowd aghast.

"This has to be a rollicking mistake!" she hissed coming right up to Franny and sticking her coral lips close as she spoke.

"Why, what's wrong?" asked Franny timidly.

"Take a look for yourself." Jody frantically waved a piece of paper at Franny. "We're being swapped! It's an error – it has to be."

"Why? Who did you fancy yourself with, fit, young Ludwig?" asked Emma, an amused grin spreading deeply across her face.

"It wouldn't have surprised me – we'd make a good team, aesthetically and...that's none of your business!"

"We'll give you five more minutes to learn who you'll be married to for the next couple of weeks and then we can regroup to discuss the details," chimed Natalie Stone, glancing at her oversized rose gold watch.

"Come on, let's go over and let them know we need to be re-swapped." Jody grabbed Franny's wrist and ushered a few people standing in their way to move aside.

"I need to see this," Emma joined them to watch the potential altercation between the management team and Jody.

"We've been wrongly placed," said Jody cutting to the chase as soon as she was close enough to Mr. Flounders to be heard.

"I'm afraid I only make executive decisions, you'll have to ask Ms. Stone. These lists are a labour of her love."

"Sorry Jody, I spent hours matching all of you using some very sophisticated online pairing methods," said Natalie

"Well I guess you don't have much else to do on those evenings all by yourself," replied Jody viciously.

"That's right. And being a single woman means I'm not eligible to be swapped for this wonderful fundraiser either. I can go home, sit back, drink my glass of wine and watch Netflix."

Jody Cresswell made a noise that best resembled a grunt and walked away.

"Now that was well-played!" said Emma, satisfied by what she'd witnessed.

"I can't believe I'm being swapped with Jody Cresswell," said Franny, feeling anxiety starting to percolate inside her stomach.

"I know, what a curveball," agreed Emma. "Do you know her husband? Please tell me he's not a bitter little fruit-loop like her?"

"Not really, he was her guest at John's fortieth birthday party all those years ago and I've seen him around since, at the school at a handful of events. We've only ever exchanged a few pleasantries. Who are you being paired with? I'm so rude, I never even asked you!"

"I'm being *swapped* with Eva and if the rumours are true about Mr. Batchford, it should be an eye-opening experience," Emma frowned.

"I wouldn't believe what Jody says..." Franny trailed off not knowing what to believe herself.

"Alright everyone, I think we're all sorted! Now I'll explain the next part of how this fundraiser is going to work," Mr. Flounders intercepted when his staff showed no signs of self-settling. "All of you who are participating in this pioneering effort will know by now, who you've been matched with."

Jody Cresswell scoffed loudly. John Webb who'd only just twigged what was happening, pulled out an unlit cigarette from his briefcase and waved in her direction to highlight their shared interest.

"Assuming you agree to it, tonight you will go home and pack to move into your new homes for the next couple of weeks," said Mr Flounders.

"I'm still not sure how any of this going to benefit the school?" said Ludwig Suneyes.

"Oh of course, sorry!" replied Natalie, tapping her chin to focus herself. "We've found a bunch of sponsors who are absolutely bowled over by the extent of our teachers' commitment to the school. Your swaps are being sponsored by strategic partners who have agreed to make generous investments into each of your discipline areas. As the wife swap is a fundraiser, parents can also pay as they wish but ultimately it's to get those sponsored upgrades for the school."

"Ah, that makes a little more sense," said Ludwig hesitantly.

"Perfect! Now, let's take Eva's swap as an example." Natalie turned to Eva, as did the rest of the staffroom. "You camping out at Emma Blue's house is going to earn the drama department state of the art staging equipment."

"I see," mouthed Eva.

"And Emma, yours will buy us a whole new custom-built recording studio!"

"That is impressive – but couldn't we have gotten the same results by doing a sponsored triathlon or something?" asked Emma.

"Heavens, no!" replied Natalie. "Running, cycling, swimming – they've all been done to death. Our market research shows that every other school in the country does that – since the end of World War Two.

"If you're going to go down that route, you're only one step away from doing a ruddy bake sale. Or declaring one Friday a non-school uniform day and asking the whole school to pay a pound to turn up dressed like the boys are all ready for one large P.E. lesson and the girls are trying to sneak off into a club somewhere.

"What we're doing – this is innovation, this is real leadership at work." Natalie smiled as if her little speech had taken her breath away.

"I guess a recording studio is a sizeable contribution," said Emma begrudgingly coming around to the idea.

"How about me, what will my swap bring?" asked Jody, springing into the spirit of competition.

"Let me see, your wife swap will get Summerfield's mathematics department brand new scientific calculators and some new software for those troublesome trigonometry problems that no one can ever really solve."

"Wait! They're worth hundreds of thousands of pounds in high-tech equipment and commercial renovations and all I'm getting are a few poxy calculators? For living with *him* of all people? You're just taking the mickey, now!" raged Jody Cresswell.

"Come on Jody, every resource is valued equally and it's not what you're worth but what each department needs that led us to ask for the calculators," contended Natalie so Mr. Flounders wouldn't have to.

"This is bullshit."

"Hang on a minute," John Webb came to life unexpectedly. "You may not enjoy calculators, though being a numbers' geek I can't think why, but as a sensitive and romantic soul I ask that you refrain from judging me until you get to know me. Besides, don't forget, we already have a lot in common." The old man held up his cigarette once more, pleased with himself.

"Oh no," said Franny at the thought that this was going to be a very long and slow two weeks.

CHAPTER THREE

The school day passed in an unsteady haze of anticipation for Franny. As though being swapped against her instincts, like an inanimate object in some car-boot sale wasn't bad enough, being sent to live in Jody Cresswell's house definitely felt like drawing the short straw. The only common ground Franny and Emma had found with Jody was that following Mr. Flounders' announcement, they'd both rigorously questioned Natalie's online pairing methods.

Another even more daunting realization began to gnaw at Franny by lunchtime. Jody Cresswell would be living in her house. She would have several days to painstakingly judge every nook and cranny of the Webb household. The home that Franny had gently breathed her love and care into over the many years they'd all resided there together. The decor would never be described as pristine or decadent but the place held many treasured memories, most of them about Ed and Lucy, Franny and John Webb's children. Despite that Ed was now twenty-one and Lucy had turned eighteen this year, Franny had carefully preserved all traces of their childhood. The various portraits that she'd sketched or painted marked each birthday and were displayed in a collage on a wall in the living room. Awards that Ed had won throughout school, for his achievements in maths and science and, Lucy had achieved for her creative writing endeavours still adorned the mantelpiece. There was a handmade height chart rendered by Franny in one corner of the kitchen, when Ed had started school. Over the years, a rainbow of markings had blossomed up the wall as the children had grown. More accurately, the diverse bouquet of colours marked only Lucy's growth-spurts reflecting her most current favourite colour, which changed every time her height was recorded. Throughout the years, Ed had doggedly stuck to the formality of a black ball-point pen to indicate his increasing height. He'd insisted that documenting height was quite unnecessary as it was self-evident how tall people were, when they reached adulthood. Still, knowing that his mother's sentimentality was the very ingredient that held the fabric of their otherwise mismatched little family together, helped him indulge the requests with a maturity that exceeded his years.

Franny imagined that although she'd always considered the home to be warm and cosy, Jody would rip it to shreds standing in the middle of the staffroom, her numerous vultures huddled around, eager to hear the next instalment of how dated the kitchen was or how the sofa sagged in the middle when you sat down.

And then there were John Webb's strange pre-occupations that would be the topic of discussion long after all the donations from the sponsored wife swap had been put to their best use. Franny was unable to decide whether it would be a disastrous event in their family history or a positive development that the old man's tedious and yet infuriating tendencies were about to be publicly exposed by the gossip queen of Summerfield School. One thing she hoped for was that it would teach her husband how easy he'd had it all these years, something she had been unable to bring across to him no matter how hard she'd tried.

"Are you all packed up then, my dear?" asked John Webb with an air of excitement in his voice that surprised Franny.

"Yes, John I'm all packed," replied Franny, gulping back some of the hurt that she felt was apparent in her tone.

"Could be an interesting experience," said John Webb, stretching loudly, ready to settle in for a lazy evening. The old man had been deeply irritated with the headteacher's idea to raise funds by disrupting his peace and quiet. However, he'd come around to the concept once he'd cottoned on that he'd be able to do whatever he pleased, including writing his beloved memoirs from the second he got home from school until he went to bed. Most of all, he was happy that he wasn't the one moving into someone else's home. Not that he didn't like living with Franny but every now and then, his hobbies were known to get him into trouble when he became so immersed in them, that they came to be detested by the rest of the family. John Webb assumed Ed and Lucy would busy themselves with hosting Jody so that he wouldn't have to bother himself with such inconvenient matters. As far as he was concerned, he'd made his best effort earlier that afternoon that Jody had snubbed. The rest was up to her. John Webb continued to watch his wife as she placed her toiletries neatly into a small overnight bag. He zoned out but was pulled back with what he assessed to be a needlessly firm stare by Franny.

"Don't want to leave me, aye?"

"You haven't asked me once how I'm feeling about our argument earlier and nor have you said you'll miss me," said Franny softly.

"Well of course I'll miss you. And about the tickets being for Prague instead of Paris, I just assumed you'd sort of come around."

"Oh, dear..." Franny gave a little sigh and continued with the last of her packing.

"I mean, if we interpret things loosely, Prague is actually known as one of the many Parises of the east. I googled it earlier today." The old man wore a self-satisfied look. Franny suffered in wretched disappointment that even he, could miss the mark by such a long shot.

"That's exactly it, John. For as long as I can remember, I've wanted to go to Paris with you. Not the many places that are comparable but the one and only Paris. It's almost worse that you chose for us to go somewhere that resembles my one dream and yet has nothing to do with it."

"Franny..."

"And you didn't choose some random place we both might have liked, you picked Prague because your idol Franz Kafka lived there and you wanted to walk in his footsteps whilst pretending that the trip was a romantic getaway for me – for us."

"But we can still do Paris one day, sweet-pea...can't we?" John Webb asked trying to summon up his predictable puppy-dog eyes, a look that had gotten him out of many self-induced jams with Franny over the years.

"Not this time," said Franny, not answering his question but instead, shrugging off his attempt to neutralize the displeasure that had made itself a little too apparent. She picked up her luggage and walked past him, into the hallway.

"I'd say please don't go but this fundraiser away from the old man will probably be the best thing you've done in ages. Take us with you?" Ed said with a playful smile, as he hugged his mother downstairs.

"Honestly, I think you're right," said Franny with a small grin as she hugged Ed and Lucy goodbye.

"Take care, mum," said Lucy warmly.

"Message me, every day. And, if you need to talk," said Franny gesturing at the old man who had dopily joined them in the living room, "just call me and vent."

"We will," promised Ed as John Webb wore a crooked, very guilty looking smile and waved at Franny.

CHAPTER FOUR

It took Franny half an hour to pull into the Cresswell's crunchy, gravel-lined driveway, after getting lost twice. When she finally found her way, she realized that the house wasn't far from her own and actually a bit closer to the school, which would be a welcome change.

Though night had almost fallen, she could see from the luminescent sconces along the front of the house as well as a distant lamppost that threw its yellow glow in her general direction, that she'd be staying in a large, extended cottage. Suddenly, Franny felt nerves. Like a wave making its way through her, anxiety started with a slight prickling on her forehead and ended up coursing down into her abdomen. She'd been so wrapped up in wallowing about John Webb's selfish ways, that since leaving Summerfield School in the afternoon, she'd not sufficiently prepared herself for living with Jody's husband.

Franny turned off her engine and sat in the growing darkness, something that always helped her to collect herself after a tough day. And this day in particular had been both difficult and twisted. She hoped that Jody's husband hadn't already been alerted to her presence by the headlights of her car in the window, as she scoped out her new environment. Although she could only just see the intricate details of the landscape that lay before her, it was plain to see that the residence was gorgeous. Compared to the simplicity of her own front garden, which she considered well-pruned when Ed got around to mowing the lawn, Franny could tell that a lot of care and precision had gone into the array of botanical wonders framing the elegant stature of the cottage.

Taking a deep breath, Franny slowly opened the car door and stepped outside. She apprehensively hoped that Jody's husband would be nothing like Jody as she silently padded over to the back of her car to retrieve her luggage. No sooner had she opened the boot, that she was startled by the front door of the home bursting open and a man, whom she assumed was Mr. Creswell, briskly jogging to meet her.

"How do you do? I'm Michael Cresswell, your new husband for the next little while!" He shook Franny's hand with a firm but comforting grip. Due to his association with Jody, that he was friendly at all, seemed misplaced.

"Hi there, I'm Franny! Your new wife for a bit," said Franny, matching Michael's warmth with a brand of enthusiasm she'd forgotten she had within her.

"Please, do allow me!" said Michael pointing at the bags in the boot.

"Oh, thank you so much." Franny followed Michael up the drive and to the front door. She passed an oval ceramic placard bearing the words, Cresswell Cottage. Entering the space that belonged to Jody Cresswell, Franny was delighted that it didn't feel like a place that belonged to Jody at all. Although she wasn't completely certain as to the kind of house she would have imagined Jody to live in, it certainly wouldn't have been this one.

"Are you hungry?" Michael asked, breaking Franny's stream of thought.

"Actually, now that you mention it, I didn't really get the chance to have dinner before I came over," said Franny tentatively, not wanting to impose, as it had gotten late. She took in Jody's husband who was broadly built, a considerable few inches shorter than John Webb. He was dressed smartly in a suit and dashing tie that boasted a bejewelled green tone, like he'd just gone to a posh restaurant for dinner himself. He was a brunette with his thick hair styled and parted to one side and had eyes that bore the depth of sapphires.

"I'm not surprised, that was quite the bombshell they dropped on you guys today, wasn't it? I imagine packing was all you had time for when you got home."

"If you wouldn't mind, would you like me to make us something – if you haven't already eaten?" asked Franny, looking around to get a hint of the general direction of where the kitchen might be. She wondered whether it was completely out of line that she'd been there less than a few minutes and asked to use it.

"I most definitely would mind," said Michael Cresswell, immediately adding, "because you must be bone tired and I should be the one offering you a nice meal – and no, I haven't already eaten, I thought we could have dinner together."

"That's so nice of you – thank you!" Franny replied, feeling her anxiety ebb away to a lighter feeling and then quickly come gushing back again for the fact that Michael's considerate behaviour was so utterly foreign to her.

"I never knew cottages had an upper floor," said Franny

as Michael carried her luggage up the flight of stairs and she followed him into the large guest bedroom.

"Traditionally, they don't. We actually had to create this by extending into the entirety of the attic."

"It all looks lovely," Franny said peering around.

"Thanks, though personally, I think it would have been easier just to move into a regular house," laughed Michael. He opened the door to one of the rooms and turned on the floor lamp in a corner of the room. The meticulously chosen furnishings perfectly complimented the décor in subtle homage to the nautical culture of the southern English coast. The room was predominantly navy-blue, mingled with a generosity of cream and gold accents that brought a femininity to the space.

"Why don't I leave you to settle in? I'll go warm our dinner, please make yourself at home and join me downstairs whenever you're ready."

"Thank you, I won't be long," said Franny quietly, as if she were expecting Jody's spectre to pop out judgmentally from around a corner.

A few minutes later, despite trying hard not to snoop, Franny found herself edging open dresser drawers and peering in, to take a good look at the secrets contained within. Each drawer was lined with pastel paper that carried a faint lavender scent. All of the six drawers were empty apart from the top one which held a few customary toiletries such as travel-sized shower gels and hand creams in elegant combinations like rosehip and vanilla.

Franny surmised that if this was the way the room always looked – which it must have, given the short notice of her arrival – then Jody might have a heart attack when she peeked around the guest bedroom, she'd be staying in. It wasn't that Franny didn't run a tight ship. The Webb home was as clean, uncluttered and organized as any. But for the fact that John Webb often diminished those attributes by his myriad habits, quirks and peculiarities, which seemed to leave their mark on every surface and nook that he came across.

Franny cringed, as she thought about a particularly weird set of thingamajigs that Jody would be sure to unearth in the dresser of her current bedroom. John Webb's gargantuan assortment of miscellaneous whistles that he'd collected over the years had at first been something that Ed and Franny had laughed about. They'd assumed it was a short-lived phase, like many others that had gone as quickly as they'd come into their lives. The whistle collection had begun harmlessly but soon, it had taken over the whole house, unchecked like a relentlessly invasive species of weed. Eventually various whistles had lain strewn about, in every room and instead of picking them up or better, tossing them out, John Webb had grown increasingly hostile if anyone so much as went near them. It was the one instance where Ed had almost come to punches with his old man because he'd purposely crushed one of the plastic monstrosities underfoot to make a point. It had been one of the few times when Franny had taken a stand too. She'd gathered up the whistles one Sunday afternoon when the old man had been out and, in her husband's words, held them captive until he'd agreed that unless he was *testing* them, the whistles would be contained in only one room of the house. They'd chosen the guest bedroom as a hiding place for the futile whistle collection because no guests had ever stayed there. Until now.

Franny freshened up and made her way downstairs, exploring more thoroughly as she walked into the immaculate living room that she'd initially glimpsed at in search of the kitchen. One stark difference from her own that immediately struck her was that, Jody and Michael had no photographs displayed. In contrast, Franny's home was decorated with portraits and artwork that showcased the four people who lived there (though Ed and Lucy were much more frequent subjects). At the cottage, contemporary paintings and prints were strategically placed to give the room the similar show-homey vibe and appeal as everything else she'd seen so far. From what Franny had gathered from all the years she'd worked with Jody and now confirmed from being in her home, was that the couple didn't have any children. Guessing that they were in their early-to-mid forties made it unlikely that their kids had already moved out.

She found her way into the kitchen, which was enormous compared to the one she was used to, partly because it incorporated the dining area as well. There was a sizeable, brilliant white island with subtle black flecks right in the centre of the room, made from one of those trendy new materials like granite or quartz. Four tall barstools made of a darkened wood and black leather were pulled neatly up to the island and above it all was a mixture of course, thick rope and wiring that held together a bunch of novelty lightbulbs, suspended at various lengths.

Franny caught sight of the impeccably laid platter before her and was sure that her jaw had dropped. The dining table to one side of the kitchen was set for two, laden with a large salad, a sliced baguette, a saucer of olive oil dotted with ruby-coloured balsamic vinegar, a bowl of fluffy, mashed potatoes sprinkled with chives, and their main, two beautifully golden chicken Kievs, that graced an iron skillet, all ready to be plated and served.

"I hope you're hungry!" announced Michael with a big

smile.

"I am – this is just marvellous! I can't believe how much trouble you've gone to!"

"I like cooking," said Michael, pleased with the reception.

"But I couldn't even smell any food when I entered your home – how on earth did you manage to whip all this up in a few minutes?" Franny took her seat and closed her eyes, feeling merry off of the gorgeous aromas.

"Actually, I began cooking the moment I learned about the wife swap. That would have been my regular time to start dinner anyway. Although, I will admit that when I heard about the special event, I got inspired. Most of it was made before you even got here. I just tossed the salad and cut up the bread as you were getting all settled – and I did brown up the Kievs, too."

"This is just...sorry give me a moment," Franny said, getting emotional. No one had ever cooked for her, specifically to this scale, since she'd entered adulthood. And, even throughout her childhood, dinner had frequently been whatever she could forage from the kitchen. A hot meal had more often than not, consisted of a can of baked beans on toast.

"Taste it before you get impressed," said Michael, enjoying the reaction his cooking had invoked.

"Is this something you do professionally?" she asked after some hurried bites, even more taken with the way the flavours played on her palette than what her eyes had discerned. Michael, poured them both a glass of sauvignon blanc and brimming with pride, tucked into his own plate of food.

"In one way, I guess I am a professional cook, as I'm the one who does all the cooking – perhaps you can relate?" he said after biting into a chunk of bread he'd dabbed into the oil and vinegar.

"Yes, I rather can! What a good way to look at it – though I can't say my own fare comes close to this," said Franny. "Would you ever share the recipe?" she asked pointing down with her fork at the chicken Kiev that was seeping out garlic butter.

"Le Cordon Bleu shared it with me so I'd be pleased to share it with you," replied Michael, fascinated by her level of interest.

"Wow – you've trained at le Cordon Bleu?"

"Trained is probably too strong a word. A couple of years ago, I did an intensive cooking course there for a few weeks."

"How was it?"

"It had been a dream of mine for a long, long time. And when I finally found myself with an opportunity to take the plunge and realize it, it was...surreal."

"I've always wanted to go to Paris and pretend I lived there, even if for a month during the summer holidays," Franny blurted before she could stop herself. Instinctively, her hand went to her mouth like she wanted to prevent any other delicately private ambitions from escaping on an impulse.

"That's a worthy dream – you should do it. You only live once, right?" smiled Michael.

"You have a stunning home, it's just gorgeous," said Franny, wanting to avoid additional talk of her own unfulfilled ambitions

"Thanks," replied Michael gazing around like he expected to notice something new to validate Franny's comment.

"So, you already know I'm a teacher at Summerfield,

obviously. But I'd love to hear about you," said Franny after there was no attempt by her dinner companion, to pick up the conversation.

"Actually, I'm not sure you remember me but we've already met on occasion at the school. And, a few good years ago, at your husband's big birthday bash."

"Of course, I do! And I'm a little ashamed that this is the first time we're talking properly," said Franny.

"You and me, both. I'm a police officer. I've been on the force, going on fifteen years now. Apart from food and cooking, I love photography.

"During my stint in Paris, I'd wake up before my cooking classes to photograph the city. Some of the printed scenes in our living room and hallway, are my work."

"Really? Wow!" said Franny becoming self-conscious of how limited her vocabulary must have sounded. She hadn't even noticed that the landscapes around her, captured Paris. She instantly speculated as to whether Jody too, liked photography and which of the prints were her handywork. However, Franny quickly concluded that the Jody she knew, didn't appreciate the creative streak in students or teachers so it was doubtful she possessed a hidden one herself.

"I too have portrayed countless parts of that city on canvas – I teach art but having yet never visited, my inspiration has been photos, images on google and my imagination," she admitted. She blamed the wine for having loosened her tongue in front of the handsome stranger she'd only just begun to get acquainted with.

"That's pretty admirable," said Michael, with sincerity as their eyes met. He topped up both their glasses and held up his own. Franny followed suit. "To us and to a happy marriage," he said winking and they clinked glasses.

CHAPTER FIVE

"So how was the first night in your new home with your new man?" Emma grinned catching up to Franny in the rapidly growing queue for morning refreshments.

"It was good," said Franny, involuntarily breaking out into a huge smile that didn't escape Emma's notice. "How about you?" she asked.

"It was very, how do I put it...interesting. Eva's husband, Bill is his name, is a preoccupied sort. He's not impolite but he's hardly the welcoming type." Emma frowned.

"Hmm, that's great," replied Franny, staring down into her empty cup.

"Alright, you. What's with that look again?"

"What?" asked Franny continuing to hold her gaze away from Emma's.

"Spill – what's going on?"

"Nothing, what do you mean?"

"You look positively uplifted, radiant even! There's something different about you and I have no clue what it is but I intend to find out before we get to the front of this line."

"It's just that, Michael Cresswell is just the sweetest, gentleman! We had an exquisite dinner, which he cooked us himself. I've never had that kind of an evening before. Not in my entire life, Emma!"

"That's wonderful - though I'm now totally confused as to how he's happily married to Jody if he's so unlike her. You know what they say about birds of a feather et cetera. What's their house like?"

"It's beautiful."

"I'm glad he put in an effort."

"He certainly did! Why, didn't Mr. Batchford?"

"He went down to the village Chinese takeaway and got us something questionably crimson-coloured, called pork balls. And, let's not forget the single chicken chow mein to share." Emma was unimpressed and Franny decided not to aggravate her further by revealing the gourmet cooking she'd been treated to.

"Men," Franny widened her eyes, not really feeling the sentiment, after her experience of Michael's company.

"I'd be interested to know how our other halves fared," Emma got hold of the kettle and began pouring Franny's coffee.

"I think we're about to find out how mine did," said Franny taking a deep breath as she saw Jody bounding up the line of their caffeine deficient colleagues and heading for them.

"Ought to be fun," said Emma with a smirk that was fully intended for Jody's viewing pleasure.

"Well, well, if it isn't the woman who got me into this terrible predicament to begin with," said a fully disgruntled Jody Cresswell.

"I beg your pardon?" replied Franny, trying hard not to reveal how intimidated she felt.

"I don't know if you're aware of it but we're in the middle of a wife swap."

"Right?"

"And I've somehow ended up in the penalty box with the world's worst husband."

"I'm sorry but how is that Franny's fault? She didn't pick you to be paired off with her husband – whom quite frankly, I feel for in this particular situation," said Emma stepping in.

"Honestly, I don't know whether the expression 'thick as thieves' applies to the pair of you more or 'thick as two planks' but that one common word certainly does. I'm talking about what on earth possessed you to marry that man all those years ago?"

"Sorry, still not sure we follow you. I take it you do know that marriage is complicated and there are a million little things that make two people come together in holy union?" Emma smiled sweetly enjoying the impact it had on Jody.

'Whatever but my point is that, had she not married that cantankerous old man, I'd never have gotten swapped to be his wife!"

"That's certainly one warped way to look at it," Emma maintained her purposefully calm demeanour but Franny, found herself feeling for Jody.

"I know John's not always the easiest person to be around," she offered, softly.

"That's completely right – he's not," said Jody, staring at Franny for additional sympathy.

"I'm sorry if your first night at our house wasn't what you'd have liked."

"It was terrible! He made me frozen fish fingers that he didn't cook through properly and squished peas."

"You mean mushy peas?" asked Emma, attempting hard to quell the laughter that was impulsively threatening to break free.

"No, I bloody well don't. Do you think I don't know what mushy peas are? My husband has trained at one of the world's top cooking schools, for crying out loud. What hers fed me last night was peas out of a tin can, that I saw him squashing up with a fork in the bowl he microwaved them in!"

"Oh dear," said Franny thinking of Michael's phenomenal chicken Kiev and creamy, whipped potatoes.

"Indeed!"

"And what would you like Franny to do about your misadventure last night?"

"Well, I...I just think she should know that..." Jody stared baffled.

"I get it," said Franny, realizing that having John as a husband was already taking its toll on her normally pompous colleague. "I'm here if you'd ever like to chat," she said.

"Thank you," replied Jody, genuinely disarmed. She moved off without another word and left Franny and Emma in peace.

"I'm not sure what to think," said Emma looking amused.

"Poor thing! But I'm pleasantly surprised that John even tried cooking her some dinner."

"I'm glad he didn't resort to frozen fish fingers and molested peas for our dinner," giggled Emma, reminiscing on Franny and John Webb's anniversary dinner a few months ago.

"So am I," smiled Franny.

"Tell me more about this Mr. Michael Cresswell," nudged Emma as soon as Jody was out of earshot.

"He's a police officer who loves cooking, so much so that he attended courses at le Cordon Bleu in Paris. And he loves photography."

"A bit of uniform, paired with gourmet cooking – very nice! Is he easy on the eyes as well?" asked Emma.

"I guess you could say, he really is," Franny said and with a blush.

"Then there are only two things I'll tell you. Firstly, how exciting! And secondly, that our friend, Jody Cresswell appears to be an even bigger bitch than we first imagined."

"How come?"

"I'd always assumed that she was sore and obnoxious because she was with someone who was equally, if not more so. Now that we're learning that's not the case, I'm inclined to think it makes her even worse for having that attitude problem."

"I think people who want to find a reason to complain will always find one and those who don't, won't."

"Well that rings true – I mean, look at you..." Emma trailed off.

"That's alright. Besides, I too have my limits," quipped Franny. What she didn't say, was how pleased she was to have an extended break from John Webb and that too, somewhere the company had turned out to be so pleasant.

As Franny and Emma walked away from their spot and exited the staffroom, Darren Easy, who'd been inconspicuously listening in to most of their conversation realized that he had procured some gossip, the nature of which would finally one-up Jody Cresswell – and not just because it was juicy but that it was about her.

CHAPTER SIX

John Webb had felt particularly annoyed the whole day after his previous evening and earlier breakfast with Jody Cresswell. The day had dragged on and as it was, he'd had no free periods. Then to make things worse, he'd had lunch duty that he'd been looking forward to for a chance to go behind the new science building and smoke. Unfortunately, it had rained which meant that every teacher on duty had had to stay inside and man their classrooms and those of neighbouring teachers.

"It's like the whole bloody universe is conspiring against me," remarked the old man as his final German class of the day slogged against the clock, to complete a mock exam paper. Normally, on the occasional hectic days like this one, John Webb would wait it out until he could retreat to the solitude of his own home where, as long as he could successfully avoid a run in with his son, Ed, there would be a couple of hours of peace as Franny got stuck into cooking everyone a nice dinner. He sighed, as he recalled how until yesterday, life was – well it wasn't perfect by any means – but it had been proceeding in its own normal fashion. He'd go upstairs and on every school day, apart from Thursday, he'd smell the familiar bouquet of moreish scents coming from the kitchen as he wrote his memoirs, completely undisturbed until food was ready and on the table.

But the day before, the old man's home had been invaded by someone who'd turned out to be a completely unwelcome visitor. And to think he'd gone out of his way to cook for her when in return, her response had been to maliciously spit out a mouthful of chewed up fish, squarely onto his precious diary that was kept on the dining table. Far from apologizing, Jody had proceeded to berate the old man for trying to give her food poisoning. She'd also told him that she'd have expected more edible food at an army mess in Soviet Russia. Ed and Lucy had been quite unrattled. The old man had sourly deliberated if pest control was his only option if he were to be prematurely rid of Jody.

The bell sounded and John Webb, immersed in an orb of self-pity, missed it altogether. It was only when one of his students named Viola Brown, stuck her hand in the air and called him loudly, did the teacher get startled into presence.

"Okay, everyone. That's it, pens down. Geez, is only one of you honest enough to alert me that you were meant to be done probably, five minutes ago?" whinged John Webb.

"Of course – because she just finished her own paper," said Anthony Stone, a pale and weedy looking fellow who sat right beside Viola.

"Not true," replied Viola Brown smugly.

"Enough, you twits! Don't you have lives to lead beyond voluntarily staying behind after school and arguing with each other? Class dismissed!"

As each student turned in their paper and left, John Webb found himself feeling uneasy about going home. He hoped, purely for his own sake, that Jody Cresswell would be a quick learner and begin to emulate Franny soon. The old man decided that maybe the reason for the disastrous evening was that he'd bothered to make such a sincere effort to welcome Jody into the home. He unexpectedly began to feel better about the situation as he twigged that Jody only got to boss him around because he'd made himself a little too useful. This evening would be different. He'd go home and act like he did around Franny. Surely, when Jody saw how he couldn't and wouldn't lift a finger for himself, she'd see the error of her ways and modify her behaviour. Problem solved, thought the old man. He picked up his briefcase, turned off the lights and whistled to himself, closing the classroom door behind him as he walked to the carpark to get his life back.

CHAPTER SEVEN

"Hello you! How was your day?" asked Michael Cresswell, opening the door and ushering Franny in with a wide grin.

"Hi! It was actually very pleasant, thank you. How about yours? By the way, I hope I didn't disturb you by ringing the doorbell?" Franny came inside and began to take off her sandals. It had been a gorgeous April day and it hadn't even rained. Although Michael had promptly given her a spare key to come and go as she pleased, Franny was a bit hesitant to just walk into a home that wasn't hers.

"Far from, I was just about to sit down to a nice cup of tea. I wasn't sure whether you were a tea or coffee drinker so I made one of each. I hope that's okay?"

"That's just perfect, I do prefer coffee so if you've already made one, I'd love a cup!" said Franny clapping her hands and following Michael into the living room. "What can I help with? Would you like me to start dinner?" she asked feeling a bit redundant.

"You can sit back and decide what you feel like for

dinner, I'll get our drinks," replied Michael going on through to the kitchen.

Franny made a quick shopping list of ingredients that they'd need for a nice, simple meal of salmon, baked in a lemon and dill marinade with some jacket potatoes and asparagus on the side. She felt a bit cheeky, knowing that her inspiration came from the terrible dinner Jody had been subjected to by John Webb the night before. At least the only similarity between her dinner and her husband's attempt would be that both involved fish and vegetables. Unlike John Webb, Franny had cooked well for many years.

The rays of the setting sun, leant a beautifully soft, golden glow to the surroundings, the room really was gorgeous. The floor was a bleached hardwood, discernible only at the edges of the room as the living space was feathered with a plush rug that resembled tufts of freshly fallen snow at her feet. There was an oversized antique bookshelf at one end, with a compact little coffee-coloured desk and chair right beside it. The coffee table in front of her was entirely made from glass with little golden detailing etched into the legs to give them a stunning uniqueness. The walls were washed a subtle shade of grey and Franny rose up from the majestic indigo sectional to take a closer look at Michael's work. It was professionally captured and yet stayed safely away from being generic.

"It's the essence of Paris without screaming it," remarked Franny to Michael as he re-emerged with a heavy oak tray that carried the coffee, tea and a platter of the most delicious looking biscuits.

"I'm glad you approve! I wanted to be subtle about it – no point in coming away with the exact same images as every other photographer and tourist on the planet, is there?" said Michael setting down the tray.

"Admittedly, my Paris art is a bit more cliché than yours, I'm afraid. I've painted many a Parisian scene that my heart has desired," Franny smiled sheepishly.

"But as a painter, no matter what you paint, you'll always put your very own heart into it. No one else will ever be able to emanate your art. Even though you take inspiration from your environment, or in your case, other people's photographs, what comes out of your paintbrush is coming from within you."

"I like your way of seeing it," said Franny, feeling tempted by the biscuits.

"Please help yourself." Michael lifted up the large plate and offered Franny.

"Oh, thank you, these look delectable," said Franny taking a circular piece of shortbread.

"My favourites, I do have a bit of a sweet-tooth so I'm subconsciously forever on the look-out for something new and delicious." Michael too, helped himself to a biscuit.

"Nothing wrong with that! By the way, I've made a list of items I'll need to make our dinner. If you could be so kind as to check to see if you already have any of the ingredients, I can make a quick run to the supermarket and get whatever we don't have."

"What a marvellous idea! But let's take a look here," said Michael, taking the list and going through it. "If you'd like to have a nice piece of salmon, we could just as easily step out to a restaurant for dinner?"

"We couldn't possibly – could we?" asked Franny getting mildly scandalized, sipping her coffee.

"Why not?" Michael covered his mouth so as not to subject Franny to any stray crumbs that might shoot out as he spoke.

"Because you cooked us such a mouth-watering dinner yesterday. I'd like to do something for you. Unless, it can be my treat?"

"It could – had you been the one to suggest it. But now it can't I'm afraid, as it was my idea so you'll have to be my guest."

"But surely as your guest, you'd let me decide on a place?"

"Well, of course."

"And if you did, then I'd insist on paying," smiled Franny, warming to the idea of eating out.

"Why don't I drive us to Gunwharf Quays in Portsmouth? It's full of seafood joints and we can see what suits our fancy when we get there?" replied Michael, ignoring the question and trying to set it up so he could pick up the cheque on a technicality.

"It's a deal," said Franny, without realizing that she'd been had.

On their drive over, they made good, light-hearted conversation. As they pulled into the underground carpark, Franny was amazed to see how full it was considering it was an early Tuesday evening.

"Hmm, how about this one, it's called Loch Fyne, so you know they specialize in fish?" asked Michael, as they strolled up to the quaint facade of a bustling restaurant.

"It looks amazing, let's do it!" smiled Franny, feeling appetized.

They went in and got a table. The menu looked ravishing and Michael quickly ordered a couple of glasses of sparkling wine as they made their dinner selections. Though Franny had initially been tickled by the idea of salmon, the vast menu made her feel spoilt for choice. She eventually settled for a pan-fried, hake fillet smothered in rosemary butter with artichokes and sautéed potatoes and Michael ordered himself the king prawn Malabar curry.

As they nibbled on the contents of their bread basket and spreads including a particularly flavourful taramasalata, Michael was pensive.

"If my memory serves me correctly, you have two children?" he finally asked.

"Yes, my son Ed's twenty-one and studying to be a marine biologist and my daughter, Lucy who's eighteen. She's doing English literature for her A' Levels, she wants to be an author one day. They're both amazing kids. Raising them has been a humbling yet growing experience for me." Franny proudly, envisioned her two children.

"I can imagine. I've always loved children and assumed I'd have kids of my own. Thought I'd make a good enough dad."

Though curious, Franny simply nodded. She didn't want to pry, knowing that decisions around not having children, either by choice or necessity, were often sensitive.

"It was Jody who didn't want them," elaborated Michael like he'd read her mind.

"The two of you seem to have built a beautiful life together. How long have you lived in the cottage?" asked Franny.

"Going on seven years."

"I'm very impressed with your sense of style – and Jody's."

"How about you? How long have you been at your current place?"

"Just a little bit over twenty-five years, actually. We moved in soon after getting married and have been there ever since."

"Wow, how old were you when you got married – fifteen?" Michael laughed but hoped for an answer as it defied his logic that Franny was any older than forty which was three years younger than he was. He'd thought her to have been the same age as Jody. But unlike his wife, he could see that Franny wasn't in the least embittered by life.

"Try a decade older than that," laughed Franny willing her cheeks not to have taken on their usual rosy hue when she felt a rush of heat go to her face.

"No!" Michael did a double take. "You're saying you're *seven* years older than me?"

"I guess I am," Franny burst into a deeply amused smile.

"But you're..."

"Yes?" Franny held off from sipping her wine lest she ended up blowing it back out and onto table. And worst still, all over Michael.

"You're stunning," said Michael, failing to think of another way to put it.

"Oh, thank you, for a woman my age?" Franny hadn't had a conversation that she'd enjoyed so thoroughly with a member of the opposite sex, ever in her recollection.

"No, not at all. You know that's not what I meant!"

"Really? And what might you have meant?"

"You really know how to corner a man. What I mean is that you're stunning. Full stop. And wonderful company. The little I've gotten to know you has been more enjoyable to me than...well let's just say, this isn't what my evenings normally look like."

The food came, looking as decadent as expected and as they both tucked in, Franny watched Michael. Perhaps because his guard was down, Franny perceived a sadness in his eyes, which to her were the colour of a deep sea with a storm coming. It was the kind of sadness that stayed hidden under a strong sense of duty and the daily rush of chores, obligations and automatic responses. It was the feeling of extreme loneliness and it was a familiar feeling that she recognized well for she had grown so accustomed to it herself.

CHAPTER EIGHT

Jody Cresswell sat at the dinner table in John Webb's house, impatiently tapping her fingernails and wearing the most unpleasant frown.

"He should be down soon," Lucy offered about her father's whereabouts with utmost politeness.

"You're just like your mother. It's uncanny how much," said Jody.

"Yes, it's something I've heard a lot," Lucy looked on meekly, not wanting to be another source of annoyance for the obviously distraught woman.

"It's not a bad thing, your mum is one of the better ones," Jody softened her tone.

"Do you miss your family?"

"That's a complicated question with an even more complicated answer," admitted Jody. "I don't have kids. Just Michael, my husband."

"Oh," Lucy shifted in her seat. Jody heard the loud ticking of the old clock on the wall in the kitchen, in the house that was otherwise quite silent.

"Are you doing your homework, then?"

"I'm writing a short story. It's more a compulsion of mine but I do find that when I write something, I can use it later as part of coursework, if I tweak it."

"Is that allowed?"

"I've never thought it isn't," Lucy smiled, relaxing a little.

"Hmm," said Jody, thinking that this was exactly why mathematics was a much more robust subject than such artsy-fartsy disciplines where anything went. No one would be able to sit and pre-emptively solve equations that could later be pulled out and used to fulfil assignments.

"I'm here, is dinner ready? What are we having tonight?" John Webb appeared, craning his neck in all directions to seek out the food that was as yet, missing.

"We were hoping you could tell us. And for goodness sake, make sure it's not the same degraded quality of meal you tried poisoning us with yesterday."

"But I normally don't...Franny has always been the one who took care of the food. Anyway, where's Ed, maybe he can whip something up for us?"

"What dad's trying to say is, as a general rule, he doesn't know how to cook. Yesterday was the second time he tried making something, at least as far back as Ed and I have been here," said Lucy, interpreting for the old man. "Ed took his girlfriend out for a meal tonight, dad."

"Oh?" replied John Webb looking flustered. "As I was saying, Franny usually puts dinner on the table and seeing as you're her replacement..." he trailed off as he saw a pair of steely eyes glaring back at him. Lucy on the other hand, unperturbed by the lack of food, had quietly gone back to her writing.

"Firstly, I may have been required, fully against my free will, to come here and tolerate this sham of pretending to be your wife but let me assure you, I'm not going to be interned to the same workhouse conditions as that poor, misguided woman!

"And secondly?" asked John Webb, stung by Jody's rudeness.

"Secondly, I want dinner and I want it now. Not the crap you tried to fob me off with last night but a real meal." Jody gritted her teeth. "I've had a hard day and I'm starving."

John Webb gazed around expectantly once more as if doing so would materialize dinner out of the ether. He tried getting Lucy's attention but she was staring down with real focus. Her hand moved across the page at an impressive speed, covering it in little squiggles. Jody continued to stare at the old man, who was trying to avoid eye-contact with her at all costs.

"Maybe I could give Franny a call and see what she recommends us to do?" said John Webb when he saw that no solution presented itself, no matter how long he sat in the heavy silence.

"You can't even figure out what to eat without your wife holding your hand and spoon-feeding it to you?" asked Jody, arching one perfectly painted eyebrow.

"Since I've been married, it's something I've never had to think about. Even when I'm away on a school trip, I either eat where they suggest or Franny packs me some sandwiches," said John Webb with disarming honesty.

"Well, that's just silly," said Jody, feeling a tad less indignant.

"How about you? What do you usually make at home for your mister?"

"How sexist of you to assume that I'm the one who does all the cooking!" said Jody, trying to cover for the fact that she'd suddenly recognized that she too, relied on Michael equally for each meal as the old man did on Franny. She shrugged off the painful fact that in this one area, she was a lot more like John Webb than she ever could have fathomed.

"We could call your old man and ask him what to have for dinner?" asked John Webb.

"No, no that certainly won't be necessary!" replied Jody hastily. The last thing she wanted to do was prove to her husband that she was so high-maintenance that she couldn't survive mere hours without his help and that too, for such a trivial decision as what to eat for dinner!

"What should we do then?" asked John Webb shuffling his feet.

"A couple of months ago, when Mr and Mrs. Blue came over and you were in charge, we ended up ordering a pizza. Maybe we could do that for tonight?" asked Lucy, looking up.

"Yes! That will do nicely!" exclaimed the old man, happy to have had his memory jogged by his daughter.

"I guess we don't have a choice, it's getting late. You order," replied Jody pointing at Lucy, "and you – tidy up, the place is starting to look like a badly run hall of residence," she instructed John Webb.

Lucy immediately pulled her phone out of her pocket and ordered a large pizza and a side of cheesy garlic bread. John Webb started moving about the place randomly picking up the salt shaker from one end of the table and placing it on the other. Having never cleaned up after himself or anyone else before, he had no idea what he was actually doing or how Franny achieved the order she did.

Jody too, retrieved her phone from the lavish black handbag that had been sitting at her feet like an obedient pet dog. She busied herself by scouring her Facebook feed for some of the best ingredients from where she could concoct the latest batch of rumours. She hid her relief that at least for one night, the food problem had been solved and she wouldn't end up with more of the dreaded uncooked fishfingers that had effectively put her off of fish for life.

CHAPTER NINE

"How was last night? Are you settling in a bit better now?" asked a voice laced with a little too much joy for so early in the morning. Jody shuddered at the sight of Franny who'd found her way to Jody before she became virtually unapproachable due to the arrival of her enormous, prattling crew.

"Err, I guess it was a shade better than terrible," replied Jody, solely because she'd been caught off-guard and hadn't had the opportunity to formulate her long list of complaints.

"Oh, that's good news! That's definitely a positive sign," said Franny, nodding along in a manner that Jody thought annoyingly cherubic.

"Actually, let's see, your husband sat there like a model of male chauvinism, expecting me to cook dinner. When I didn't, your daughter kindly came to his rescue and engaged the services of one of those mediocre high-street chains to bring us a pizza. I couldn't tell you whether it was Pizza Hut, Pizza Pizza or Dominos because it took all I had to chew through the cardboard like base they'd used. And then, your dearly beloved made a big song and dance of having tidied up when all he did was re-arrange the chaos."

"John tried to tidy up?" asked Franny, surprised.

"I had to instruct him that the house was beginning to look like a bombsite, of course. And in the process, he managed to throw out my vaporizer!"

"I'm so sorry, is that like an inhaler, or something?"

"No, I use it to vape!"

"Vape? I think I've heard of that, it's like smoking isn't it?" Franny asked with intrigue.

"Yes – Jesus! Anyway, I woke up this morning and I desperately needed to clear my head before coming here and when I asked if anyone had seen my vaporizer, your precious John scratched his head and said he may have discarded it last night, assuming it was a broken dog-whistle!" Jody breathed loudly as Franny continued to stand patiently and hold up her side of the bargain about being there to chat. Her gaze then fell upon what was in Franny's hand. It was a Tupperware box full of delicious breakfast pastries and she instantly knew where they'd come from.

"But it's plain to see that whilst I languish away at your husband's bachelor pad, you're having no problem moving in on my home," Jody gestured to the croissants.

"Oh these – isn't Michael an amazing chef! Please do have one!" Franny opened the box and heartily offered the goods.

"Hmph," replied Jody, quickly grabbing a crescent-shaped pastry, not even waiting for their conversation to end before she heartily bit into it. She had begun to miss the overly sensitive and emotional Michael, who had become little more than a cook, housekeeper and whiner over the years. Or perhaps she just missed food for the fact that she'd had no breakfast available to her at the Webb home. She stared openly at Franny, who seemed a touch too secure with herself and the situation – almost like that offering had been like a subtle but potent signal, that Michael and his baking were now her territory. Jody felt like an outsider, looking in on her own life, as it slowly receded away from her.

"As I said, come on over if you need to chat," said Franny, spying Emma entering the staffroom and saying her goodbye to Jody, quite unaware of the rabid glare aimed at her.

"Ah, those look tasty!" said Emma, helping herself as Franny offered her friend a treat from the box.

"Poor Jody, she seems to be having a really tough go of it," said Franny.

"And you look like you have a wholly different tale to tell," winked Emma.

Franny felt herself flush, something that had become increasingly common since she'd become acquainted with Michael Cresswell.

"How was your evening?" she asked, to defer the question.

"Same old. He's a drab sort, our Bill. We ate Tesco's own brand of macaroni and cheese and talked about little more than the weather. I do think Jody is onto something with the gambling though."

"Oh?" said Franny wanting to stay out and yet, allured.

"After I'd finished watching Coronation Street, I went over to the study to bid him a good night before I went upstairs to run my bath. The man was at his computer screen with a very complicated looking spreadsheet. It had about fifty tabs."

"That could have been anything though, couldn't it?"

"It was all colour-coded and I glimpsed something about

net profits. All I know is that it made me nervous and it wasn't even about my finances!"

"Oh dear, poor Eva – and Bill. It takes desperation to get into that sort of trouble. And we don't know what their circumstances might be that led him to make the decisions we think he makes," said Franny, thoughtfully keeping her voice as low as she possibly could.

"You're absolutely right." Emma agreed tearing a strip off of her croissant and rolling it into a bite-sized portion. "Mm, delicious! Did you make these?"

"I wish! It was Michael – he's an utter genius in the kitchen."

"And does he know you have such a soft-spot for all things Parisian?" Emma raised an eyebrow with a suggestive smirk.

"Why, yes but..."

"Ah-ha! This wife swap just got interesting!"

"No, it didn't. I have no idea what you mean!" said Franny, utterly embarrassed.

"Okay, riddle me this: what did you two do last night? I bet it wasn't eat mac' and cheese out of a sodding can."

"Fine, we went out. To a place named Loch Fyne in Gunwharf Quays."

"Fancy! Charlie and I love that place! Seems to me, that this Michael chap likes you a lot, missy! And who wouldn't? You're smart, genuine and smoking hot."

"Emma!" Franny gushed, never having imagined that such provocative adjectives would be used to describe her.

"I'm serious! And he's obviously used to the big, cold, cruel world type of a lifestyle with Jody. You'd be a breath of fresh air to anyone."

CHAPTER TEN

For once in her career, Franny spent the morning not able to fully concentrate on each of her students as they filed into her class and she instructed them of their assignments. The last class before lunch was her year seven group and although she'd initially set them the calm and ordered task of completing still life drawings from the contents of their pencil cases, ten minutes in, she felt too alive to let her students engage in such drudgery.

"How about you each pick your favourite song and draw what it means to you?"

"I'm not sure what you mean miss?" said a small girl with a dainty blonde ponytail to one side.

"Oh, sorry Rebecca, hmm – how can I explain it better?" Franny thrummed her pencil on the table as she pondered what exactly she meant. The idea had come to her spontaneously and felt like it would be a lot of fun. Beyond that, she hadn't really analysed or anticipated what she expected from the finished pieces. True to form, she chose to be honest.

"Today, the assignment I set you, was to make still-life sketches of your pencil cases and everything inside them."

"Yes, it is boring," said Rebecca with a grin.

"I agree. You see, for me, even though it's important to develop skills, including with still-life portraits at some point, the real idea of art is above all else about self-expression.

"We often pick songs that suit our personalities, dominant mood and feelings. I thought it would be an enjoyable detour for each of you to pick your currently most loved song and draw whatever it makes you think and feel."

"Do we need to draw what the lyrics say?" asked a boy named Johnny who sat at the other end of the room from Rebecca.

"If that's how you interpret the song, then sure! And if the song has no lyrics or it makes you feel something different from the lyrics, you can draw that. There are no limits from me. It might even be a certain colour that pops into head as you think about it. Anything you like, just have fun, that's my only criteria."

"That sounds wicked!" said Johnny. "Can we listen to the songs on our phones to remind us how they go?"

"Actually, I think it would work better, if you all close your eyes, and think of the song. You can hum it to yourself if you like. That way, you'll be able to access the deeper feeling that comes with it," said Franny with a chuckle.

"Can we paint instead of draw?" asked Rebecca.

"Of course, dear, if that's what you'd prefer."

The class was still for about two minutes and then as students began preparing their materials, a low-volume chatter began. Franny considered what song she'd choose as her favourite. She smiled softly and decided it would definitely be something either by Sam Cooke or Cliff Richard. She was pretty sure that none of her students would know either, as much as she too, only had a vague idea of the popular artists who were busy leaving their mark on young hearts and minds.

Franny made her way around the classroom giving words of encouragement as she saw interpretative endeavours taking shape. But her own mind was occupied with the beating anticipation of returning home in the evening to a house and husband that weren't hers. She'd never been one to look outside of her own life for greener solutions to her challenges but what had become clear to her in the past few days was that she had a lightness that made her look at life like anything was possible. Just being around someone who actually asked her about her day and listened when she spoke was truly therapeutic. Franny deliberated if this was what Emma and Charlie's relationship was like on the inside – it certainly appeared that way to her. Perhaps there were two types of husbands in the world where one kind was like Michael or Charlie and the other, like John Webb. Then Franny remembered what was being said about Eva Batchford's husband and concluded that maybe there were more than two sorts of man after all.

The class concluded without much ado and her students seemed pleased as they handed in their achievements. Franny decided that she'd include the music interpretation assignment in future classes. She was sure Emma would approve and maybe it could even go the other way, where students could think of a particularly moving piece of art and make music about it in Emma's lessons?

Lunchtime was all about the *Grease* rehearsals for Eva

Batchford's production of the show. Franny made her way to the school's main assembly space, Townsend Hall. Under one arm, was tucked an over-sized canvas that had been given a red background, with the *Grease* logo painted boldly in the shape of a vintage car whose outline was apparent in white. Emma was already waiting there, as was Eva. A few students sat cross-legged on the stage with their packed lunches open in front of them.

"We're taking the first few minutes to eat and discuss how things are progressing and what we hope to achieve with today's practice," said Eva, biting into a piece of pizza she'd picked up from the canteen.

"Right and I've been thinking about the dynamics of "Summer Nights" and it might be better from an auditory standpoint, if our Sandy and Danny stand up-front on the stage where they'll have access to the stronger microphones than if they file in, singing from the side entrances at the back of the room, like we were doing last practice," said Emma getting straight to business. She saw Franny and welcomed her with a grin.

"That sounds fair," replied Eva.

Franny sat down cross-legged with the students and unpacked her sandwich and an apple from her lunchbox. As her main role was to create fifties-themed artwork with her students after school, the meetings weren't compulsory for her. But she attended most of them as they helped her really get into the musical and in turn, feel confident that the props being produced under her guidance accurately depicted what was required. Although Franny had always been partial to *Grease* and had been at the screening done in Eva's classroom when the cast had first been selected, she'd still gone back and watched it in minute detail a few more times to get her head around all the flamboyant paraphernalia that her student volunteers would be creating.

"Franny, your painting looks great," said Eva, sipping from a carton of chocolate milk and turning to Franny for an update.

"Thank you! It was done by a very talented young lady in one of my year nine classes – I'll pass along your praises, she'll be delighted. We were thinking of displaying this as signage, just outside Townsend Hall to get everyone into the spirit."

"What a good idea!" said Eva. "And how are the costumes coming along?"

"Very well, we've finally come up with a way to give all the pink ladies instant silver hair rollers for the performance of "Beauty School Dropout"."

"That's amazing, how?"

"We've already started working on a number of silver hats, shaped like cones, with Styrofoam curlers, wrapped in foil that go up the lengths. That way, the girls can very easily whip them on and off for the number."

"I can't wait to see!"

Franny finished her sandwich and as students took their places to rehearse "Summer Nights" reflective of Emma's advice, she softly hummed along to herself and noted that Eva seemed to be enjoying the latest rendition.

"Well done everybody – that was amazing! We still have a few days to go but if we all keep working at this rate, we'll give the West End a run for its money!" Eva dismissed the students, thanking them. She exhaled, running her hand through her short hair and leaning back against the wall.

"Tough job?" smiled Emma.

"Tiring but I love it," said Eva.

"And, how's my husband treating you?" asked Emma

getting to what really fascinated her, as soon as the last student had closed the set of doors behind them.

"Good," said Eva. Franny thought she saw her flinch at the question.

"Glad to hear it. If you need anything at all, just let Charlie know, he'll see you right," continued Emma.

"Oh okay. We don't really talk much," said Eva and walked away before Emma could say anything further.

"She seemed evasive," said Emma to Franny, quiet taken aback.

"She doesn't seem to take kindly to anything she thinks of as private, I think," suggested Franny, inwardly finding Eva's behaviour needlessly abrupt.

"It's not like my Charlie not to talk to someone who's a guest in our house."

"No and I'm sure he's been perfectly hospitable," said Franny feeling for Emma.

"I'm beginning to think it's us – or me. Maybe she just doesn't like me."

"No, I'm sure it's not personal."

"She didn't even ask me how I'm doing with her husband, who incidentally is very uncommunicative and appears only to know how to hang out with an excel spreadsheet!"

"That might be why she's so touchy," offered Franny, lightly rubbing Emma's back as they got their belongings and headed out. "It could be that Charlie is everything she wishes Bill was and it's too difficult for her to think about being back home so she just blocks it out." As she said the words, Franny hoped she was speaking only about Eva and not inadvertently about herself too.

CHAPTER ELEVEN

"How is everything, my dear?" asked John Webb, catching up to Franny as she headed to the carpark.

"Great! How are things with you, John?" said Franny as she reached her car and fumbled in her handbag for the keys.

"Absolutely, things are as expected. Jody is one demanding lady," the old man put on his best, most pitiful looking face.

"Why? No, don't tell me, she doesn't actually expect her meals to be made for her, does she? Or, wait, does she expect you to help out with the housework?

"In a word, yes." The old man's eyebrows rose epically, meeting in the middle to resemble an arrow pointing upwards.

"No!" Franny chuckled, feigning outrage as she unlocked her car and waited to hear what the old man really wanted so she could get a move on. Sure enough, John Webb didn't fail to deliver.

"I'm at a loss, really. I mean, I don't even know what the

woman eats and on top of that, she's just so whingey . What would you make, if you were ever to cook for her?"

"Ah, I see. Is this you asking me for ideas, my dear?"

"Maybe a little," John Webb gazed down at his feet, coyly.

"Okay, well I think we have two issues to explore here," Franny humoured. "Firstly, what does Jody like to eat? Is she vegetarian, or vegan or even gluten-free? And secondly, are you up to the challenge of cooking *any* kind of meal, no matter how complicated or simple?" Franny wasn't perturbed in the slightest that her husband had sought her out only to ply her of ideas on how to deal with Jody Cresswell's dietary needs – not because he missed her.

"Right, my thoughts exactly...and if you were to guess, what do you think might be the answer to these questions?"

"I think it might be easiest, if you just ask her about that first one, dear."

"Okay, and what about the second?"

"Seeing as, to my knowledge, you've never cooked a meal in more than twenty-five years, that's a question only you can answer. I expect that it might be helpful if you were to go with some simple recipes and follow them exactly."

"Well, yes that's what I thought too. Anyway, good chat," said John Webb. "I expect you must be feeling like a fish out of water? It must be tiring having to go to a strange house and figure out all the chores as well as having a quandary similar to mine of cooking for a complete stranger?" John Webb had already crossed his fingers behind his back hoping for a similar report from his wife.

"Actually, John – and don't take this the wrong way – it's like being on a wonderful holiday."

"Oh?"

"Michael is a phenomenal chef and has treated me to

his gourmet cooking. And now that you mention it, I should ask him how to split housework but to be honest, and maybe it's because they don't have children, their home is spotless."

"Just my luck, I had to get stuck with the worst wife in the world. Oh Franny, do you have any idea how hard it is to put up with someone as annoying as her?"

"None whatsoever," said Franny ironically.

CHAPTER TWELVE

Lucy answered the doorbell and instantly shrank back from the guest who looked eager to engage. His dark hair had been carefully blow-dried into an exaggerated but somewhat scanty quiff. He wore oversized glasses with a slight tint that Lucy had seen on her father from photographs of his youth, several decades ago. As the man held out his hand to shake hers, Lucy spotted a host of rings and a chunky silver bracelet on his wrist. She didn't generally dislike many people or professions but one type of combination that was most mismatched with her docile personality was the door-to-door salesperson. She found it impossible to be unkind enough to slam the door and walk away when faced with one. As a result, Lucy had ended up spending her money from the various part-time positions she'd held since the age of thirteen, on a host of superfluous goods. These included everything from glittery eye make-up she never wore and double glazing a year after the windows had been freshly done, to a troupe of sponsored dogs, cats, ferrets and donkeys.

"I'm so sorry, I'm not really looking to buy anything –

and we were just about to sit down to dinner," said Lucy taking a big, deep breath and chiming out what Franny had patiently rehearsed with her a few weeks ago, after she'd learned that Lucy had signed them up for a new boiler service and paid a year in advance to a company that no one had heard of before.

"My apologies, lass! Gosh, do I really look like one of those used car-salesmen types?"

"Actually, you look like a door-to-door sales type," said Lucy, confused that she had to be the one to reveal what the stranger was doing at her door.

"Oh Lord, that's no good, is it? I'm Barry – Barry McGuinty – I'm actually a prestigious news reporter for the British Broadcasting Commission. I pick up the non-urgent stories, you know, the feel-good ones that actually touch lives and help build real and lasting communities across Great Britain,"

"Oh, you mean the BBC?" asked Lucy, wondering if the eccentric man was who he claimed to be. She briefly thought she should offer him some directions in case he was lost, although she was certain that his phone could give him better directions than she could.

"Indeedy. Anyway, I've been led here to interview the two teachers from Summerfield Community School who are involved in the Wife Swap Fundraiser program." Barry McGuinty held out his identity-card attached to a blue lanyard for Lucy to inspect before continuing.

"Oh, now I understand! You're here to see my dad and Mrs. Cresswell – in that case, just one minute, I'll go and get someone for you," said Lucy relieved to be able to hand Barry off.

"Hi, there! I'm Jody Cresswell, please come in, we've

been expecting you!" said Jody, keenly shaking Barry's hand and taking him through to the living room.

"Barry McGuinty, pleased to meet you. Very nice little family home you have here," the man said, scanning his surroundings.

"Hmph, it's not mine – I'm the one who's been swapped into this home with my colleague, her name is Franny Webb. She's currently living it large, in my house."

"It's a perfect home though. Of all your colleague's homes I've visited so far, this is the closest to the kind of environment we'd want to work with. It's got that viewer appeal to it, just look at all the personal stuff. Makes a house a home, don't it?"

"I guess," Jody wrinkled her nose, not sure if it was the surprisingly gruff calibre of the reporter or that the Webb household, which was in stark opposition with her own would be showcased as the idyllic setting. "What's the process, I take it you ask us some questions?"

"It's been going a few days now, hasn't it – this fundraiser? Why don't you – and Mr. Webb, is it? – talk me through how you're both finding everything? I have to say your headmaster has a novel idea. With any luck this'll give us the kind of numbers we've come to expect from the reality genre. It's always a winner." Barry settled himself on the sofa, opened his rucksack and got out his laptop, camera and tripod and began setting up.

"I think I can give you the juicier part of the picture –"

"Yes, yes, how about we do a run through of everything over a nice cup of tea?"

"Lucy, could you get the gentleman a cup of tea, please?" said Jody. Lucy nodded obediently and went to the kitchen.

"She's the Webbs' daughter, right?"

"Yes."

"What great hospitality!"

"I'd leave the judgment about the wider family until you've spoken to John Webb – but yes, I am growing fond of Lucy. She's a lot like..." Jody trailed off.

"Like who?"

"No one." Jody sat there instantly conflicted. On the one hand, she found Lucy so like Franny. Franny. The woman she'd always admired as a teacher for her wholly amiable personality. Someone who'd never needed to light fires under others to go by her day with an understated power that came purely from grace. And now, Jody had even grown to admire Franny's ability to remain married to a maddening man like John Webb. To be able to do so took no ordinary level of tolerance but one that surpassed any she'd ever been acquainted with. However, Franny Webb who was quite marvellous for so many reasons was also now suddenly enjoying the warmth of Michael Cresswell that Jody hadn't in too long. And as if that wouldn't have been tempting enough, Franny's basis of comparison was John Webb. Jody shuddered, as her insecurity – that Franny and Michael were an inevitability – surfaced without warning.

"Have you spoken with the wife, Franny Webb, yet?" asked Jody, wanting to know how best to position herself for the upcoming inquisition.

"Not yet, no. If things go well here, I'll just get her story and those of your other colleagues at the school. It'll be good to have that juxtaposition between this snug abode and that of the establishment for which this fundraiser is being run." Barry lit up as Lucy came through with a tray that held two cups of tea and a small plate of Rich Tea biscuits.

"I asked dad to come downstairs. Hopefully he

shouldn't be too long," said Lucy, placing the tray down on the old wooden coffee table in front of Jody and Barry.

"Thanks, Lucy," said Jody, sincerely. She watched Lucy move away and for just a moment, she felt a sense of pride akin to that which Franny often felt, from being around a benevolent young lady like Lucy.

"Should we begin and your makeshift husband can join us when he's ready?" asked Barry, helping himself to a biscuit and giving it a slow-motion dunk into his tea.

"Yes, that's probably for the best, though I can't think what he could be doing up there."

"Okay then, just ignore the camera and think of it as a casual chat with a friend."

"Alright," replied Jody, primping her curls in preparation and quickly reapplying her flaming coral lipstick. She admired her reflection in a small, circular compact mirror that she'd pulled out from a side-pocket in her handbag.

"I'm here with Mrs. Jody Cresswell, a teacher at Summerfield Community School. Like a handful of her colleagues, Jody is participating in a very unique way to raise money and get sponsorship grants for her school. Jody is part of a two-week wife swap with one of her fellow teachers.

"She's currently living in the home of Mrs. Franny Webb who's swapped homes with her. In this segment, we'll also be catching up with Jody's new husband but first, I have a few questions for Jody." Barry paused the recording and reached for another biscuit. "Are you ready for a few questions about your arrangement?" he asked, as he munched.

"Yes, shoot," said Jody trying to refrain from showing her annoyance that the man thought it perfectly acceptable to be mumbling with his mouth full. How unprofessional, she thought.

"Jody, thanks for inviting me into your new home."

"A pleasure," smiled Jody.

"How is everything coming along?"

"Well, that's a loaded question, Barry. First of all, let me say this. I think our headteacher is a visionary. His idea is wonderful in spirit, I'd go as far as saying, it's fantastic. And for some of my colleagues, I'm sure you'll see that – how do I put this – being swapped is an enormous step up from what their real lives look like."

"And that's a loaded answer! How about you? Has your experience been what you expected?"

"It has. And that's what's so shocking to come to terms with to be honest."

"Oh?"

"Yes, I've known my colleague Franny Webb for many years now. And her husband John, whom I've been paired with, also teaches at Summerfield School. Over the years, we at the school have come to know John and Franny as quite a pair – they seem to be a good fit for each other."

"And how are things coming along with you and John? How do you like being Mrs. Webb?"

"Can you see my new husband anywhere? That's how things are coming along. He's absent, narcissistic and expects me to do all the cooking, cleaning and housekeeping – in a house that I'm not even familiar with!"

"Oh no, that doesn't seem fair." Barry put on a look of concern. Jody couldn't discern whether this was genuine or routine theatrics.

"It's fine – his wife and my colleague, Franny, seems to do well here," Jody said, motioning at their surroundings. "I think she even enjoys the way this man behaves. I don't want to second guess but..."

"But?"

"There are certain situations in life, where we need to nip things in the bud and when we don't, we're equally responsible for when things get out of hand. I don't think Franny has ever nipped anything in the bud in her life. Perhaps she's just too nice."

"Oh my. It seems that things have already gotten quite intense in this wife swap! Maybe you've stumbled in on something you weren't quite prepared for or familiar with?"

"Absolutely. To recount my experience in a nutshell: I've had fewer meals at that table over there than I've spent days under this roof. John Webb expects me to swoop in and cook and other than that, he utterly ignores that I exist. Now, I may have been swapped but I'm pretty sure I'm still in the twenty-first century. Only it's hard to keep track of that here."

"I guess that *is* what makes a wife swap spicy ain't it? The diversity of the experiences. Why don't we take a look and see what...good grief! What's that noise?" Barry got up and paused the filming once again, peering all around to try and locate the origin of the sound.

"No idea but I can bet I know who's responsible," said Jody standing to attention with her arms folded across her chest. She proceeded up the stairs and Barry followed her with his camera rolling. She turned right at the top of the staircase in the direction of the din and threw open the door to the guest bedroom, where she was staying.

"Oh hello," said John Webb, looking pleased. The bed and both side-tables were covered with what, upon closer inspection, Jody determined were small, plastic whistles. The old man held three of them in his hand. They were clearly the culprits of the distorted and high-pitched noises that had been heard moments ago.

"What the hell are you doing in here?" asked Jody, surprised and peeved by the weird ritual that was being carried out in her room.

"Allow me to introduce you to the wonderful world of whistles," grinned John Webb.

"Why?" asked a flummoxed Jody. Barry stuck his head into the room, both with a view to introduce himself and to capture the strange scene.

"Think of it as an alternative to the boring and ordinary woodwind instruments, namely, the flute. I play these on a weekly basis. And who are you?" asked John Webb, raising a questioning eyebrow at Barry and his handheld recording equipment.

"That makes absolutely no sense, these whistles aren't exactly woodwind instruments!" Jody stared hard at the old man.

"Pleased to make your acquaintance – I'm Barry McGuinty from the BBC. I'm covering the wife swap story for your school and I'm here to peer into how everything's going. Don't mind me, I'm just going to set up back here and join you both on the other side of the lens."

"Nice to meet you. I'm John. A. Webb. Budding author and eclectic hobbyist."

"I can see! And Jody was just telling me that you're a fellow teacher at Summerfield?"

"Oh that. When the need arises but obviously, I intend to leave my mark in other, more esteemed ways than my stint at that school." John Webb gestured to the room and began blowing another set of whistles.

"Case in point, see what I'm having to put up with?" asked Jody indignantly.

"John, so far what would you say has brought you closer to understanding the kind of home and life Jody comes from?"

"All I know, is that Jody likes to sit at the dining table for long stretches and goes on her phone as an intense hobby."

"What the blazes?!" sneered Jody.

"And when dinnertime rolls around, we're all equally at a loss as to how to proceed. I was even chit-chatting with my real wife, Franny, for suggestions after school today. Jody seems a tough nut to crack – she doesn't say much about what she does at her home and yet she's always narked about something or the other. Very unlike what I'm used to, if you ask me, which you did." John Webb smiled on a job well done, while Jody huffed loudly.

"And Jody, at this stage, what have you gotten out of being John Webb's wife?" asked Barry, ignoring the oddly lopsided atmosphere of the room, where John Webb was quite at ease, even amused by the situation and Jody was undoubtedly irate.

"What I've gotten is that I've learned there are men out there who never should have been married to begin with. And frankly, I'm mortified that as I'm left to rot here with...*him*, while his wife, who's used to the thankless task of living with him, is off having a lark with *my* husband."

"In fairness, I still need to speak to Franny – and Michael, isn't it, your husband's name? I'll be getting their story soon." Barry smiled, a nuisance smile that was wholly fake and ever ready for his camera.

"What's to get? Look at what this man is doing? He's spending his evening blowing into a cacophony of moulded, plastic! By going into my home with my husband, his wife has been upgraded from rags to riches overnight and I'm being starved by this maniac and manhandled by his stupidity!"

"Strong words, from this brave wife," said Barry, gazing directly into the camera.

"And that's not all – you should both know something. My gut says, Franny is there right now, trying her charms on my Michael, probably crossing her fingers as we speak, that she can make her so-called temporary charitable position, a permanent one. The woman's after a better life and thanks to me, she may just have found one," Jody sniffed away tears that weren't really there.

"Wife swap – a boldly different way to raise funds for an already well-endowed school, or a frivolous way to wreck otherwise happy homes? We'll surely find out in the second half of this program – stay tuned." Barry seemed like he'd struck gold with the inadvertent mud-slinging that had provided a deeper angle to the story he'd assumed would be about a straight-forward fundraiser.

John Webb shook hands with Barry, who delightedly agreed to show himself out. Jody thanked him for coming. As soon as she heard his footsteps recede downstairs, she returned to the guest bedroom and began grabbing the whistles and shoving them into an old white, carrier bag she'd found in the airing cupboard on the top of the stairs.

"Wait a tick! What are you doing to my precious whistles?" said the old man making an attempt to snatch back his whistles that were quickly disappearing into the bag.

"What do you think? I'm throwing them out, they have no use other than to clutter up my room!"

"Oh no, you most certainly aren't!" the old man tugged desperately at the bag.

"Yes, I am! I'm teaching you a lesson that Franny should have taught you a million years ago!"

"Let my whistles go! Give me the bag!"

"No!" Jody viciously seized the remaining few whistles off of the bed and disappeared downstairs as the old man howled. She paid no heed to him and was soon out on the curb, shoving the carrier bag into the wheelie bin for garbage collection in the morning.

CHAPTER THIRTEEN

Franny awoke with the sun streaming in through a gap in her curtains. She instantly smelled coffee being brewed in the kitchen and smiled, stretching out on the bed. It had been three days since the debacle at the Webb household and with wife swap half way through, Franny had had one of the most perfect weeks of her life. Her weeknights had been a mixture of a few evenings spent in the invigorating company of Michael and a couple spent relaxing at the cottage by herself when he'd been on night duty, policing.

Yesterday had been Saturday and Michael had had to work most of the day. Franny had made herself useful by doing the weekly grocery shopping and cooking for the two of them later in the day. She'd decided upon a nice, home-made lasagne and as she'd layered everything up in a glass dish, she'd felt a pinch of guilt, that she couldn't remember when cooking had been so enjoyable. It wasn't that she didn't love cooking for or feeding her family. But the fact was that Ed now ate many meals outside the home and Lucy was only a mild, albeit very welcome presence. Franny found that no matter what she made each day, it was guzzled with such pre-occupation by her husband, that the effort almost seemed in vain. Once or twice, to see if John Webb had even been aware of what he'd consumed, Franny had asked him after clearing away, what they'd eaten for dinner. His answers had all been wildly incorrect. When they'd had spaghetti, he'd recalled shepherd's pie. And when dinner had consisted of jacket potatoes, topped with sweetcorn and tuna, the old man had guessed at a pork roast. Only being around Michael, had Franny begun to discover how exhausting it was being unnoticed.

In the afternoon, Franny had met up with Ed and Lucy for lunch in town, in a quiet little café. She'd hugged them both tight, realizing how very much she'd missed seeing them over the past few days.

"How are you both holding up?" Franny had asked as they'd chomped on their paninis.

"Okay," Lucy had grinned, her usual even-keeled self.

"Wonderfully," Ed had smiled, surprising Franny.

"That's great – how?"

"Because for the duration of your absence, I've moved out too," had been the reply, helping Franny make sense of her son's demeanour.

"Where are you staying?" she'd asked, instantly worried.

"In a temporary room at the halls of residence in the university. Students can stay there on a short-term basis if there's a transition or they face hardship in their current housing situation. And I'd call mine a hardship of huge proportions."

"As long as you're safe and happy," Franny had smiled with relief.

"Trust me, mum. I tried. Ask Lucy, the first night was hell. I can't study or live with those two nutjobs. You're the only reason I live there. And, of course I'm there because of you too, Luce." Ed had said as Lucy had given her brother a somewhat hard stare. "But you know how mum manages to handle dad and mute most of his behaviour by the amount of support she gives us. I can't deal without her in the picture."

"How about you Lucy, are you really okay?" Franny had said, concerned for her daughter, whom she wished for once, hadn't been blessed with her docile personality in combination with a strong medical prescription that helped keep her qualms away.

"I'm doing well, mum. Jody means well. She's nice to me. And dad...well he stays busy – normally ducking for cover from Jody," Lucy had replied, with an amused look.

After they'd parted ways, Franny had wondered if Michael would have minded for Ed and Lucy to come over for dinner that evening and then immediately discounted the idea picturing how John and Jody would cope, alone.

Franny finally rolled out of bed and got dressed. She made her way downstairs and was greeted by a jolly song, coming from the kitchen. It stopped a soon as she made an appearance.

"Well, good morning, you! Did you sleep okay? I hope I didn't wake you when I came downstairs?"

"Morning! Not at all, I must have slept in," Franny stifled a yawn and eyed the coffee pot.

"Sit down, I'll get you a cup."

"I thought you preferred tea?"

"I do but I love a good cup of coffee too. And all the better when I have company." Michael smiled, handing her a steaming cup and bringing over two plates, garnished with scrambled eggs and toast. "The jam and butter are on the table, I shall join you in just a moment."

"Thank you this is truly wonderful," said Franny tasting the eggs, which were made to perfection, with thinly chopped up chives sprinkled on top. "What's your secret?"

"Lots of cheese." Michael placed two glasses of freshly squeezed orange juice down on the table.

"What genius!" said Franny, who loved cheese in all its different forms and varieties.

"I'd really like for us to spend the day together," said Michael sitting down and taking a sip of his coffee.

"That would be marvellous," said Franny, reigning in her rather wide, involuntary grin. "I've already done the week's food shopping so please let me know whatever else needs to be done and I can get stuck in."

"Yes, because my plan was to sit back and watch you indulge in a bout of slave labour. I'm joking, how can you possibly think that's my idea of a Sunday well-spent? Besides, does it look particularly grimy to you in here?"

"No, that's not what I meant," said Franny, her brown eyes flashing in self-consciousness that she'd just insulted the cleanliness of Michael's home.

"I know, you were just being your sweet and helpful self."

"Did you have anything in mind – for today? Is there something special you like to do on Sundays?" asked Franny thoughtfully, pondering on whether perhaps Michael and Jody were churchgoers, something her own family had neglected since Lucy had been baptized all those years ago.

"No, for us, or at least me, weekends are just a blur of work. I work most weekends, actually on both days."

"Oh, is that common on the force?" asked Franny.

"Mostly for those of us who are unmarried or divorced," Michael stopped and they sat there for a minute or so, saying nothing.

"I find staying away from home a bit longer to be a good solution too," said Franny, wanting to break the silence.

"You have good instincts, don't you?" said Michael, referring to how Franny had read between the lines about him and Jody. "But I can pick up extra shifts. How do you stay away when school ends so early, each day?"

"I've been offering an extracurricular art class that I hold every Thursday after school. Students are free to work on art projects from class if they wish or do something completely different that inspires them."

"You're an amazing woman, Franny Webb," said Michael, biting into his piece of toast.

"I don't know about that," replied Franny.

"You are. I can tell that your husband is no easier to get along with than my wife."

"Hmm," Franny nodded. This was something she could definitely vouch for, though there were immense differences between her old man and Jody. John Webb was self-pitying where Jody was good at victimizing others. Also, Franny was quite certain that Jody knew how her wagging tongue affected those around her and John Webb was completely oblivious of how his actions had any consequences.

"How do you picture that those two are getting along?" asked Michael.

"Jody and John? It's hard to say, they've never really had much in common at school," replied Franny diplomatically.

"Enough about them. You asked me if I had any ideas about today and I do. How would you like to do a pottery class with me this morning? It's something I've always wanted to try but have never gotten around to it.

"Please tell me honestly, if it's something that doesn't

appeal or if it's too close to your day job being an art teacher, I promise I won't be offended."

"I would love to!" said Franny, excitedly. "I've wanted to try it too. Summerfield's been trying to get a pottery wheel for the last decade and it always falls through, somehow."

"Okay, I don't want to rush you but as soon as we've finished breakfast, we should get going. I've already booked us a class for this morning, in case we wanted to!" said Michael, enthusiastically.

CHAPTER FOURTEEN

"How was your weekend, Emma?" asked Franny, blowing on her hot coffee and settling herself in a corner of the staffroom, ready to catch up.

"Good God, it was the longest weekend I've ever had – and with my younger daughter, I was in labour for two whole days." Emma looked put out.

"I'm so sorry to hear! What happened?"

"Bill is *the* most boring person in the world! That spreadsheet is the raciest thing about him. I swear I can totally see now, why he got into gambling – and the ensuing debt. Without his troubles to keep things exciting, he'd flat-line." Emma hushed her voice into a whisper, retaining her astonishment.

"He actually has a stamp collection. But not an active one, no. One that he collected when he was a teenager. Yet, because so little has happened in his life since then, it has pride of place at the dining table, where he fondly peruses it during dinner, each and every night!

"Then he watches Match of the Day over a pale ale and if it's not airing that night, which it's mostly not, the man watches reruns!" Emma took a deep breath and stirred her tea.

"He seems like most men in England if he's obsessed with footie," said Franny happily. "But if you ask me, I think he bugs you so much because you miss Charlie."

"Of course, I do! We talk everyday but it never dawned on me that I was married to my best friend until I lived with someone who's so unlike him. How much of a cliché are we?"

"If you are, it's in the best way possible," said Franny, involuntarily thinking of Michael first as someone she could see herself being best friends with. She tried shaking away the notion but Michael had so much in common with her. They were such different people on the surface and yet, in one short week, Franny had found that she shared much with the burly but gentle-spirited police officer. She did a quick mental tally that they'd had more deep conversations in the past few days than she'd had with her own husband since Ed and Lucy had been born.

"How about you? Are there any interesting developments on your end?" Emma winked, "Or have you uncovered something wildly irritating about Mr. Perfect?"

"Oh, Emma, I never said he was perfect! But if you must know, my weekend was...absolutely spectacular."

"Dish up!"

"Saturday was a quiet day and I met Ed and Lucy for lunch which was wonderful. Then I made us, Michael and I, dinner and he loved it! He really relished each spoonful."

"Poor darling! I almost forgot what John's like," said Emma breaking into a smile, happy for the different perspective her friend was getting. "Then what happened?"

"Yesterday we did a pottery class together – something we've both wanted to do for ages!

"We each made a mug – of course, my attempt was the most amateur thing you'd ever see. I ended up with something resembling a squashed cabbage rather than a mug."

"How did Michael's turn out?"

"It looked like a real mug!"

"I'm sure yours did too," Emma laughed. Talking to Franny always made things better. "Have you thought about what will happen after this week is over?"

"We'll end up with one lop-sided mug and one clean, well-sculpted one," Franny smiled, knowing fully that Emma wasn't talking about the mugs.

"No, I mean, will the two of you stay in touch?"

"I – I have no idea," said Franny, apprehensively. "I hadn't really thought that far ahead yet. I guess now that I think about it, I'd love to – platonically of course. He's such a smart and interesting person – and he loves to chat."

"You really think your connection is platonic?" Emma smirked.

"Emma, of course! I'm married and Michael has Jody! He'd never look at me as anything other than a good friend."

"That's exactly my point and I've said it before – he has *Jody*. How happy could he be? And the two of you are off creating beautiful ceramics together, I'd say that's more than a touch romantic."

"And on top of everything else, he's seven years younger than me!"

"Yes, because no one ever gets attracted to someone with an age difference. The law is crystal clear that you can only fancy someone born in the same year as yourself." Emma was enjoying their catch-up as immensely as Franny was.

"Hello? What about John?"

"Look, I admire your loyalty. If anything, I'd say you're the meaning of the word. But..."

"But what?"

"Don't get offended but..."

"Yes?"

"John doesn't know what he's got with you."

"I'm inclined to think you're right. With Michael it's just so splendid having someone to talk to – about art and cooking and life. Oh, look at me carrying on – you must obviously think my normal life is as invigorating as Bill's!"

"Don't worry, Bill is in a league all by himself," assured Emma.

"And what league is that?" asked Eva, who'd been getting herself a cup of morning coffee and caught the tail-end of their conversation.

"Uh, none, we were just talking about how much we've both been enjoying wife swap. Bill's great," Emma tried redeeming herself.

"Saying, *he's in a league of his own* doesn't sound like things are great for you," said Eva, turning a shade of beet-root that clashed with her hair in the most unflattering way.

"No, I'm not saying it badly but you've got to admit, all he does is fiddle with that one spreadsheet and watch Match of the Day."

"And?"

As Franny watched the two women verbally duke it out, it occurred to her that Eva was protesting Emma more out of being wounded that her reality with her husband had been summed up so accurately.

"Wife swap has been a real mindbender for so many, hasn't it? And if you ask me, perhaps our points of tension come from feeling homesick deep down, in some way, even if we're not immediately aware of it," Franny said, trying hard to smooth over the friction.

"Right, that must be it," said Eva in a way that convinced no one, least of all, herself. She walked off, giving Emma a final, hardened stare as Natalie Stone came looking for Franny.

"How are you ladies doing?" asked Natalie, in her friendly and yet fully business-like tone.

"Very good thanks, how about you?" said Franny as both her and Emma nodded pleasantly, mindful that management didn't make conversation due to any genuine curiosity about staff wellbeing. They paused, waiting for the real reason to surface rather than to get any insight into Natalie's day-to-day life.

"That's great, I was hoping to have a quick word," replied Natalie, checking her watch and then gazing at Franny.

"Of course, I hope everything is okay?" asked Franny.

"Yes, yes, marvellous. As Mr. Flounders had mentioned at the beginning, we're being covered by the BBC and as it turns out, the wife swap is drawing in more interest than we expected.

"We're getting a segment on the evening news that's double the length of what we'd initially been allocated." Natalie's face gleamed boastfully.

"That's good isn't it?" asked Emma.

"It's wonderful! There's a reporter about our premises for the next couple of days and he's doing dedicated coverage of the fundraiser. Franny, I'm not sure if you knew, but I'm told that your home is being showcased as the main off-site setting that's being used – so congratulations – and be ready because you'll be of particular interest!"

"Oh wow, has John already been interviewed then?" asked Franny, feeling nervous.

"Yes, as has Jody. Their story really seemed to hit the spot and the reporter wants your side of things right here at the school."

"Okay," said Franny with a growing sense of apprehension. If Natalie picked up on it, she showed no concern and instead became engrossed in skimming through her new emails on her phone.

"Anyway, must run, lots to do! I swear, most days this job feels akin to being rung out by the spin-cycle of a gigantic washing machine. Just go, go, go!" And with that Natalie Stone left the conversation as brusquely as she had entered it.

"What does she mean by your side of things?" asked Emma a bit cynically, smoothing down her bob.

"I don't know," said Franny, beginning to feel ill at ease.

CHAPTER FIFTEEN

"Ugh! Did you see her in the staffroom this morning?" asked Jody, coming and seating herself awkwardly on John Webb's desk, just as his class funnelled out.

"Who are you talking about?" asked the old man moving across the room and distractedly shoving some textbooks into an already burgeoning filing cabinet.

"God! No wonder your marriage is dissolving before your eyes – Franny! Your wife!"

"What about her?"

"It's been more than a week. Have you even checked in and asked her how everything's going?"

"Well, no. I did briefly chat with her last week but to be honest, I was too worried about what to feed you for dinner to ask how she was. She seemed fine. If anything, I could tell she'd been missing me."

"What gave you that idea?"

"She was happy to see me. It was the end of the day and she was waiting to get in her car and leave and she had a big smile on her face ."

"How did you figure that was because of you? Did it

ever dawn on you that she might have been happy to be getting *away* from you and going back to her new living situation?" said Jody through gritted teeth.

"I've never had a problem with the ladies," said the old man, coming over to his desk and standing next to Jody. "I mean look at me, I'm a dapper gentleman. It's a classic case of the wants."

"The wants?" asked Jody, confused.

"Yes, the women want me and the men want to be like me. But alas, no sale. In the case of the former, I'm a married man and in the case of the latter, I'm a one-of-a-kind mint edition." John Webb said, pleased.

"Exactly how stupid are you?" spat Jody.

John Webb raised his eyebrows at the unprovoked verbal assault.

"Your wife is fully smitten with my husband!"

"What makes you say that?" The old man closed his tatty briefcase, that had been gaping open with its contents strewn across his desk, like a gutted fish.

"How long have you been married?"

"Twenty-five years and counting, of pure marital bliss. How about you? Less I presume, especially the blissful part?"

"Do you know anything about your wife?" asked Jody, shuddering with great effort to ignore the old man's comment directed at her.

"If I was being modest, I'd say I pretty much know Franny inside out."

"How are you so cocky, you dense, old man? Your wife, whom I only know as a colleague and likely have a darn sight more insight into than you, tolerates you out of some mysterious, self-deprecating need to be nice.

"If you treat her even a tenth like you do me, I guarantee that she's trapped in a lonely and unhappy marriage with you. Because let's face it, what could she *possibly* get from you?!"

"What are you insinuating?" asked John Webb, offended.

"I'm saying that thanks to your winning ways, by the end of this week, neither you nor I will have a marriage left to go back to," said Jody, distraught, whereas the old man felt victimized by how he'd gone from leading a quiet, if slightly boring life, to having his marriage sabotaged by a stupid fundraiser.

"Oh!" the old man's life as he knew it suddenly flashed before his eyes. He contemplated if just maybe, this was Jody's way of trying to set up some kind of pre-emptive deal, that on the exceedingly off-chance that Franny walked out with Mr. Cresswell, Jody might be able to set up shop with him.

John Webb had always imagined he had a sweet deal with Franny. And yet because Franny had been his first and only girlfriend, he'd known no different. It had never struck him that taking a woman like Franny for granted was the worst possible course of action in securing his own good fortune.

"But if, for one minute, or maybe thirty seconds, we assume what you're saying is true about my sweet Franny, surely your husband wouldn't also walk out on you?" he asked.

"It's not that simple," Jody flinched.

"Why not?"

"Michael and I have our problems," she swallowed a lump in her throat that was hardened by pride but concealed anguish within.

"Oh Lord, what should we do?" asked John Webb,

trying to keep his desperation under wraps. There were no circumstances where he could see himself ending up with Jody Cresswell. The woman would be the end of him. Even given another week or two, she'd not only starve them both, but totally snuff out his writing career by working him into the ground.

"You need to do exactly as I say, from now on. We need to watch Franny carefully and at the end of the week, when that Barry what's-his-name comes back to do his final interview with us, we need to be ready."

John Webb nodded because what hadn't escaped even him about Jody Cresswell, was that everyone's business was her business and when she talked, she was usually onto something.

CHAPTER SIXTEEN

Franny reached Cresswell Cottage and placed her handbag on one of the hooks in the carefully arranged closet near the kitchen. She glanced around the space at some pricey looking bags in an impressive array of tones lining the small wall upon which her own paltry bag was now suspended. The custom shoe cubby along the bottom of the closet too, held several pairs of some of the prettiest shoes and sandals she'd ever seen, most of which were so spotless that they couldn't have been worn more than half a dozen times. They were the types of shoes that Franny had never learned to walk in and had given up trying since she'd turned thirty. She pondered how her colleague could afford such luxuries but the thought was fleeting and she stopped herself as other people's finances were none of her business.

She couldn't see any signs that Michael was home but nor did she spot any notes from him saying he'd be away for the night. She didn't recall him mentioning that he had extra duty tonight but assumed that extra shifts probably came up if units were short-staffed. Franny perused the living room and her eyes fell upon a photograph that she'd missed as it was tucked away in the corner on a side table. She picked it up and was surprised to find that a considerable amount of dust had collected on the gilded frame. It was the only item in the entire house that had been ignored. She blew at the frame and cleaned away the rest of the grime with the edge of her dress. The photo revealed a younger, dapper Michael in his police uniform. She held the picture up to take a closer look and noted the same smile that slightly creased the edges of his eyes. The picture was the only one of its kind in the whole house insomuch as that it told a story of the life of one of the home's occupants. Franny placed the photograph back down in a more prominent place on the same table. She envisioned how interesting it must be to be married to someone who worked in a totally different career. She found it fascinating how each of her colleagues (apart from her husband), led such disparate lives from one another and yet Summerfield brought them all together.

Franny went into the kitchen to make herself a cup of coffee and was just about to start dinner when she heard the key turning in the front door.

"Evening!" called Michael, cheerily. He swiftly headed upstairs to change.

"Good evening!" said Franny, retrieving another cup from the kitchen cupboard and making Michael a cup of tea.

"How was your day?" asked Michael.

"It was superb. Although, there's a reporter who wants to interview me at some point this week about the wife swap. How was yours?"

"Oh dear, will you tell them of all the terrors during your stint being married to me?" asked Michael with a cheeky grin.

"I'll say that I was lucky enough to be paired with an absolutely delightful young man," said Franny, looking in the fridge for dinner ideas.

"Young – ha! Sorry but who are you talking about?" Michael laughed as he sipped his tea and pulled open the dishwasher to begin emptying it.

"Well you are young – at least compared to me," Franny blushed. "Did you have a good day?"

"I did. I was mostly catching up on my admin today. And don't get me wrong, I love my profession but if you want the truth..." Michael trailed off, glancing at Franny and then quickly looking away. "What would you like for dinner?"

"I'm flexible, what do you feel like? Sorry, what were you saying?"

"Nothing...it's okay, I guess I've forgotten."

"Wow, I really love your spice rack!" said Franny opening up one of the cabinets and picking up a few neatly labelled bottles and inspecting them in awe.

"Do you like spicy food?"

"I do. Although, I have to say, I like food that uses spice as part of its flavour profile more than food that's just spicy and has no other seasonings to it, if that makes any sense?"

"Ah, got you. Like a true artist you like a complex flavour profile – like a painting that's been layered with colours gradually, rather than been washed with one bright colour."

"That's exactly what I mean!" said Franny, impressed.

"Okay in that case, I've got it – I'm making chicken fajitas for dinner and I'll stir-fry the vegetables in different seasonings from the ones I'll marinade the meat in. You'll see! If I succeed, the flavours will all come together – with just that bit of a kick."

"That sounds scrummy!" said Franny. "But only if I can help you."

"Of course, but don't feel obliged. If you're tired and want to put your feet up, I won't mind in the slightest."

"Never, this may be one of my only chances to learn Mexican cooking from a French-trained chef!" Franny rolled up her sleeves. Michael handed her a white apron and put on a navy one himself.

"Judging by your gastronomic delights, you're a gifted cook – have you ever taken courses?" he asked, running some red and green bell-peppers under the tap.

"Oh my, no! I just love food, all the fragrances and textures – and how every fruit and vegetable can be prepared in so many different ways. I've always found cooking to be a very immersive process. I know what I'm about to say will sound silly but since I heard about your training at the Cordon Bleu, I haven't been able to stop thinking about it."

"Why is that silly?" Michael asked peeling away the skin of a red onion and bracing for his eyes to water.

"Because I'm making plans about a city I've never even been to," Franny smiled.

"That's alright! Gives you all the more reason to finally make it happen!"

"Would you ever do another course there?"

"Absolutely! Maybe we can go together someday?" Michael stared intently at the chopping board as he diced up an assortment of vegetables.

"Wouldn't that be a treat! Do you think we'd ever convince John and Jody?" Franny smiled, pulling a pack of chicken breasts out of the fridge and preparing them for the marinade that Michael had already begun stirring together.

"I'd never convince Jody – and I'm not sure I'd want to."

"Oh, I am sorry, are the two of you having problems?" Franny had suspected that something was off in the Cresswell's marriage soon after she'd been swapped. She never heard the gushing reflections of Jody that she'd first expected but she'd thought it was because perhaps Michael was a private person. Many who were skilled in the social graces found it difficult being showy about those they truly loved.

"You could put it that way – although really, it's just the same few problems over and over that have fuelled resentment."

"I feel for you. If it helps, I think every couple goes through ups and downs," suggested Franny.

"I'm not even sure anymore, where our ups ended and our downs began. The first real issue started with the topic of having kids," said Michael, tenderly handling the chicken and fully covering each piece in the marinade.

"You said before that Jody didn't want them," said Franny, realizing that it was something Michael had likely been wanting to get off his chest. Maybe if he told her, it would spare him from saying something he'd regret to Jody.

"We met when we were both in our mid-thirties."

"How did you meet?" asked Franny.

"At one of Portsmouth's marine heritage festivals. We hit it off immediately. Before I met Jody, I'd had a few relationships here and there but nothing lasting. I loved Jody's feisty side – she was so brutally honest. Other women I'd been with were experts at saying what they thought I wanted to hear but with Jody, I really thought things were different.

"Early on in the relationship, we had the big chat – we both wanted a family and were in it for the long-haul. We got married in less than two years of being together and soon after, our problems began."

"You don't have to tell me if you don't want – but I'm listening if you do," said Franny suddenly feeling that she was betraying a bond that she never knew she had with Jody. She wasn't sure if it was even about Jody or whether she found it sad to see her own image of Jody's life, crumbling with every sentence Michael spoke. And yet, her fondness for him made her want to listen and console someone who'd become dear to her so quickly.

"I want to. I need to say it aloud," Michael sighed. "I thought that given our ages, we'd start thinking about a baby as soon as we were married. But whenever I raised it, Jody would brush it away and shut me down. A couple of years passed and Jody made it obvious she'd changed her mind – she was no longer interested at all."

"Do you know that for certain, or was it just something you stopped talking about with her?" asked Franny.

"She once told me that after day in and day out of teaching other people's ruffians to add and subtract, she didn't need to come home to her own."

"Oh dear," said Franny feeling Michael's pain. She had no idea what she'd do without Ed and Lucy. For all that children needed from parents in their formative years, her children had given her the most selfless love and trust she'd ever had. And there was no denying whatsoever that for her, it was a love incomparable to what she had with John.

"Yes, oh dear indeed. Had I known beforehand, unfortunately no matter how much I loved someone, unless they couldn't have children for reasons outside of their control, I'm afraid to say it would have been a deal breaker for me. As far as I'm concerned, Jody hoodwinked me." Michael retrieved a heavy skillet from underneath one of the kitchen counters and began heating it on the stove, adding globs of olive oil.

“Why do you think she did that? Maybe she didn’t want to lose you?”

“If you’re thinking it was because she loved me too much to let me go, I think that’s a very selfish reason. I don’t think love is about trapping someone by lying to them. Its about risking that you’ll lose them by telling the truth.”

“I can’t argue with that,” said Franny, stunned by how much conflict so-called happily married couples carried inside of them.

“And the real kicker is, that I thought after dropping the circular conversation about kids, she’d be happy. But instead, she just became more distant and bitter – I’ve never understood it. Over time, what I thought of as Jody being warm-blooded just became Jody being rude and immature. Did you know, she talks about absolutely everyone at your school?”

“I did get that sense,” said Franny picking her words carefully. She didn’t reiterate what she really thought most days, which was that Jody was an archetype of bitchiness.

“Please let me know if I’m out of order but I’ve heard a lot about John too,” said Michael. Franny discerned the same tact in him, where he sought to learn whether or not there was any truth to what he’d heard.

“It would have surprised me greatly if you hadn’t,” said Franny, cracking into a smile. She watched Michael sauté all the ingredients together and begin to warm some tortillas in another shallower pan. “Most people talk about John.”

“He seems like a colourful character,” Michael too, lightened up.

“You could say that,” said Franny. “To be honest, people often come and complain to me about him, just because I’m there. The top-ranked question is, how I put up with him. I've heard whispers about how people assume that we're the odd couple," admitted Franny.

"Based on the rumours I've been party to, from my wife, your husband is a bit eccentric. Based on my first-hand experience of you, you're absolutely nothing like him."

"I think that John's heart is...it's probably in the right place. But he always puts his own dreams and wishes first."

"Do you miss him, since coming here?" Michael whipped out a couple of plates and began setting the table atop the huge island in the kitchen, laying the cutlery down perfectly, like he was preparing a table at a high-end dining venue.

Franny studied how finesse came so naturally to Michael. In what seemed like the distance but was really only a few feet from her, she could hear the sizzling of the marinated strips of chicken that had been added to the pan. Everything smelled delicious and yet, Franny's mind had wandered away from the impending dinner.

"I'm afraid I find that a very difficult question to answer."

"Why?"

"Because if you're asking if I've found myself longing to see him and be in his company at any point during my stay here so far, then the answer is no. Not because I'm not fond of him but because he's been oblivious of me in the past two and half decades."

"How have you stayed with him so long?"

"At first, I busied myself with his pre-occupations – we watched all the movies he loved, enlisted ourselves in various hobbies that were dear to him back then, and a curiosity to me. I saw it as part and parcel of getting to know

John better. Then we had kids and I became immersed in raising them..."

"And what about now that they're all grown up?"

"I've cultivated my own interests and hobbies. And I've found a very good friend – a teacher at the school." Franny wore an inquisitive expression, analysing her life was a bit scary but there was something freeing about it.

"I guess my marriage to Jody started at that point – where we were already both deep into our own lives. Maybe too much to really be attentive about what the other person might want."

"It's never too late to change that," said Franny genuinely believing it for others.

"What's your story then? How come things are the same as they've always been for you?"

"I guess it's because we've been together so very long – and John's just John. He's always just there. He's unusual, there's no doubt about that, but I never thought that should be something I, nor anyone else, should hold against him."

"The way I like to look at it, is whether you'd miss the person if they were gone."

"How about you, Michael? Would you miss Jody if she was gone?" Franny asked, not knowing if there was a correct answer to her question.

"I've asked myself that frequently, during the last few years. And yet I never knew. Until last week, when you walked into this house and showed me what it's like to actually want to come home from work every day."

Franny felt her face flush and instinctively put her hands up to her cheeks, half expecting to hear them sizzle just as the food had done minutes before. She'd never been in such an unfamiliar situation before. Franny quickly told herself that it wasn't her presence that mattered to Michael

– it was Jody's absence that had made the home an all the more welcoming prospect.

"I think you're just lonely?" she asked, hoping that her words weren't patronizing.

"I won't lie to you – I am. I have been for a long time. But trust me when I say that coming home to you has showed me what a marriage should be about. We have so much in common, our art, the cooking but that's not what gets me."

Michael plated the food and as they ate a hearty and delicious meal, Franny slowly began to grasp that until now, she had managed to successfully avoid bringing up those very feelings that had been laid bare, in the middle of Michael Cresswell's kitchen.

"You've done a beautiful job with the fajitas," said Franny.

"Thank you. You know, this is exactly what I'm talking about," said Michael, once he'd finished a bite. "What's opened my eyes is that I've seen what it's like to be the same as someone. We both go out of our way to make it about the other person. We care. And Jody has certainly never made anything about me. Since our first meal out together, with Jody, it was always about her. I didn't think it mattered."

"And how do you know that somewhere deep inside, Jody doesn't truly love you?" asked Franny, Michael's words giving her a further revelation about her own marriage.

"Love doesn't mean anything unless the other person feels loved," said Michael, smiling sadly. "I believe that you'd be inclined to agree," he added taking her hand in his. As their eyes met, there was a tenderness between them that Franny was sure she could easily lose herself in.

CHAPTER SEVENTEEN

Franny stood at the edge of Townsend Hall, watching the props her art students had worked so hard at, being put into action in a rehearsal of *Grease*. A year eleven who was playing Frankie Avalon, smartly belted out "Beauty School Dropout" and the costumes for the back-up dancers appeared to have come together exceedingly well.

"She won't even look at me!" protested Emma, gesturing at Eva Batchford who was at the opposite end of the room.

"She's not really looking at anyone apart from the dancers," soothed Franny.

"No, I can feel it, she's avoiding me that little bit extra. I've tried approaching her thrice since she caught me talking about Bill and she can't get away fast enough. I swear, this wife swap is straining relationships all over the place."

"What do you mean?" asked Franny.

"Ooh, I heard earlier today, that Jody Cresswell is completely on edge!"

"Why?" asked Franny, feeling at least in part, culpable about Michael and Jody's problem.

"I wanted to tell you but I didn't want you to worry – I promise you were the first person I wanted to share it with," said Emma.

"What is it?" asked Franny with unease creeping into her.

"Don't look so terrified, it's nothing you've done! Heavens it's not even something John has done, for once. I heard Darren Easy placating Queen Cresswell this morning in the staffroom, quite loudly, I might add. Jody was blubbering away. She seemed to think that there's a very real possibility that you and Michael will run off together by the end of the week!"

"Goodness – where does she think we'll go?"

"No idea, but you know what? I think she sees you as a real threat!"

"But I've done nothing to make her feel that way – that I know of," Franny wracked her brain. "I hope I haven't given the wrong impression. I know that things weren't too smooth between her and Michael but still..."

"Wow, really? Has Michael said something?" Emma's eyes lit up.

"Oh, I shouldn't have said anything," Franny groaned. "It just comes across in some of the stuff Michael has said over the last few days."

"Doesn't surprise me. Unless she's a total sociopath, she's probably as obnoxious to him as she is to everyone else who crosses her path. I even feel for John, having to put up with her for these last several days."

"I wouldn't go that far," said Franny with a smile. She clasped at the slightest possibility that Jody's presence would finally straighten her old man out for when she moved back home.

"Your musical arrangements are off," said Eva coming over to confront Emma. A few of the students glanced across at her and inconspicuously nudged each other.

"Oh, really? I was very impressed with how everything went," said Emma softly, attempting to diffuse the tension.

"No, I'm not sure where you pulled that score from but the tempo and pitch weren't what they need to be for an upbeat musical. It sounded like some kind of re-imagined version of *Grease* if it were a tragedy."

"Okay, I can go away and check that and let you know what I find. Though I must say, I don't expect to find too much seeing as I photocopied all the sheet music from one of the official songbooks. My arrangements are the original ones used for the movie and all ensuing musicals." Emma frowned, unsure exactly what the issue was but deducing that the root of the problem lay elsewhere.

"Right you are!" hissed Eva, bunching next to Emma and Franny, out of earshot of the students.

"I'm really not being funny but I can already assure you, the instruments are tuned perfectly and the sheet music *is* correct. If there's anything that's off, maybe we could look at the choreography together?"

"I bet you'd like that wouldn't you – to pick holes in my area of expertise?" argued Eva Batchford, shedding any semblance of the docile persona that Franny and Emma had come to know.

"It's got nothing to do with that and this is far from personal for me – you're the one that has the problem with how things sounded, not me!" said Emma, whose voice too was a whisper but her tone had tightened up.

"Of course, now I'm the one with the problem?"

"Ladies, if it helps, I heard the song too and it was just lovely, as was the dance sequence," said Franny coming to the rescue.

"Thanks, Franny. Then again, you find everything *just lovely*, don't you – from badly arranged musical numbers to other people's husbands."

"Alright Eva, I think that's quite enough!" hushed Emma. "You've made it clear that your grievance has nothing to do with the musical at hand but I would have thought that at least you'd have the professionalism and common courtesy to do this away from impressionable, young minds!" Emma headed out, nodding at Franny to follow her and do the same.

CHAPTER EIGHTEEN

Franny sat at her desk, feeling distracted. Her year ten art class continued with its coursework in the background, intermittently asking her for help on certain techniques. As their projects were on a broad topic called 'Exploration', the themes and content of their work was of a very personal nature – something Franny fought hard to bring into every item on the curriculum list. No matter how banal the mandatory pieces she came across, she'd always find ways to make them of significance to her students. The last thing she wanted was for her young protégés to deem art as monotonous. Over the years, Franny had learned that if a teacher could be just a little inventive with the interpretation of the assessment requirements, the national curriculum gave a fair bit of leeway to what could be classed as acceptable study.

She rubbed her temples, squinting towards the door. She could almost swear she'd seen John and Jody through the glass window but as soon as she thought she'd glimpsed them, their faces were gone. She got up and walked over to the closed door, staring hard, all the way down the empty hall. She frowned beginning to think she was seeing things. Franny cringed, remembering what Eva had said earlier in the day.

"Miss, are you okay?" asked one of the students, whose exploration project was about the depths of the ocean.

"Yes, thank you dear. Just a bit of a headache," replied Franny, sitting back down in her chair.

The truth was that whichever way she cut it, Franny was attracted to Michael. She had been since the day she'd pulled into the driveway of Cresswell Cottage and come face to face with the man's hospitable warmth. He was the opposite of her husband and, unlike for someone like Emma, this was a welcome change. Franny had completely forgotten what it was like to feel the way she did when Michael was there. She unconsciously raised an eyebrow, questioning if she had ever felt how she had in the past few days. That airy sense of wanting to skip through the empty halls when everyone was in their assigned class and actually doing it. That flutter of wings in her stomach when she was driving back to the cottage, especially when she knew that Michael wouldn't have a night shift. Until the last, almost two weeks, each day had been the same as the last, with the weeks, months and years all melding together to make one long, yet reduced life.

At the other end of the art department, John Webb and Jody Cresswell silently skulked outside, having scaled the hallway at a record speed to avoid being sighted by Franny. Jody had a free period but the old man had been rudely taken from the middle of his class, having been burst in on by Jody. She'd convincingly announced that there had been an emergency involving a member of the Webb family. As soon as she'd successfully extricated the old man and they'd turned the corner, she'd explained to him that they were about to indulge in some good, old-fashioned spying on Franny Webb.

"Why?" the old man had queried, scratching his head.

"Because this is where she'll be her true self, when she's in her element, teaching," Jody had replied, looking John Webb up and down with palpable disgust.

When they'd approached Franny's crammed classroom where students were hard at work, both Jody and John Webb had been taken aback by the order Franny was so effortlessly able to maintain.

"You mark my words those sods would have been massacring each other in one big paint fight had that been me sitting there!" John Webb had shaken his head in disbelief.

As they came away from the serene sight, Jody sighed loudly and rolled her eyes.

"Now, what did you get from that?" she asked.

"Well, I guess Franny's been blessed with a good set of students – her job isn't half as stressful as mine, no wonder she puts in extra hours!"

"No, you moron! God! Do I have to spell everything out for you? She was deep in thought. Like she was using that art lesson to evaluate her life and choices," said Jody looking agitated.

"Really? You got all that from Franny doing a bit of day dreaming – like I do, in truckloads each day?" the old man said unconvinced.

"I'm a woman, we know these things. My intuition said she was plotting her next move. Who's the new man in her life?"

"Mister Jody?" said John Webb, thinking quickly.

"Good, his name's Michael but at least you're catching on – finally!"

John Webb held back calling the notion preposterous, that two weeks was enough to have such a life-altering impact on all four of them. He winced at the tiniest prospect that he might end up becoming mister Jody number two.

"No thank you!" said the old man aloud, leaving Jody flustered, as he took off for a cigarette to help calm his nerves.

CHAPTER NINETEEN

"Hi there, are you Francine Webb?" called out a strange looking man, walking in Franny's direction as she made her way to the car. It had been so long since anyone had referred to her so formally, that she kept on walking until she heard the surname.

"Hi, actually it's Franny," she replied, stopping, "do we know each other?"

"No, but we will very soon. I'm Barry. Barry McGuinty from the BBC, I'm covering the wife swap story and I was hoping to get a few moments with you for a chat," said Barry, thrusting out his hand.

"Ah, of course, yes. I was told that there will be a reporter wanting to talk," said Franny courteously shaking hands. "When are you free?"

"Now as much as ever," said Barry. "The venue however, could be better. I've scouted out all the locations on offer at Summerfield and I've spoken to a few of the other teachers in the gym, the cafeteria, even in the music rooms."

"How about my classroom, it's a nice little nook with lots of work done by my budding artists?" suggested Franny.

"Hmm, that sounds interesting but I was thinking Townsend Hall? I've scoped it out and there are some very inspiring works up in there related to *Grease.* I assume there's a musical taking shape?"

"Sure, that's an excellent choice. Actually, even those props were handmade by our students so your idea will be a subtle yet delightful way to get a bit of publicity for the school and our upcoming musical," said Franny excitedly.

"Good stuff, why don't you lead the way?" Barry adjusted his heavy backpack and followed Franny. "It's quite an impressive school, ain't it?"

"Yes, our head is very diligent about maintaining the facilities," said Franny, feeling like a tour guide. "Have you interviewed a lot of the staff who are participating in the fundraiser?"

"A few. But to be honest, your story interests me more than others." Barry regarded Franny curiously as they reached Townsend Hall.

"Why's that?" asked Franny becoming wary.

"Because I went and interviewed your other half and that other lady, Jody who teaches here, at your home."

"Oh right, of course!"

"I only went there because that day, I was running behind schedule and by the time I got to Summerfield, all you teachers had gone home. I'd visited a few of your colleagues' homes, and I was convinced that school was the only place for the interviews to take place. Nothing stuck out about any of those houses. But still I wanted to at least pop over and have an initial chat."

"Oh?"

"Yeah and then when I went and saw your house, it was

such a warm and fuzzy location that I decided to film right there and then, discounting most of the other interviews. These things have a way of coming together on the spot."

"Thank you, I'm honoured you felt that way." Franny blushed.

"After meeting your husband, I can see that all credit goes to you," Barry laughed.

"Thank you!" said Franny, thinking herself flattered whilst at the same time, quite curious as to how things had panned out with her old man.

"Why don't we plonk down over in one of the seats over there and that way it'll give an impression of what the place looks like after hours? With conscientious staff like you buzzing around, still working hard for the pupils, even when they're not here?"

"Sure, whatever you think is best," said Franny, sitting down in one of the multitude of seats in the first row.

"Okay then." Barry propped his camera on a table he'd pulled over from the side of the room and took a seat, to the left of Franny. "Camera's running, just ignore it, I've got another, less obvious one here with me so we can get a couple of different angles to work with in editing."

"Okay," said Franny, trying hard to steady her voice which was as frayed as her nerves.

"So, Mrs. Webb, along with your husband, John, who we spoke to earlier, you've been taking part in the wife swap to raise funds for Summerfield Community School."

"Yes," nodded Franny.

"And how is it all going so far? What are the highs and lows of being a swapped wife?"

"Well, I'd say it's a very original move by our head," said Franny surprising herself by how scripted she sounded. Natalie would be proud.

"Yes, no doubt there. But how about your own personal experience? How does it feel to be married to someone else for two weeks? Hopefully he's treating you well?" Barry winked at the camera.

"Absolutely, it's been a very enriching experience, all in all," said Franny involuntarily getting a smile across her now rosy cheeks.

"Sounds like there's a story there! At least that's what my sources tell me?"

"Erm, I guess there is. It, err, it turns out that I've met my new husband before and actually getting to know him, has been a very positive experience," Franny tried hard not to divulge too much about either Michael or the joy she'd had by being with him, which Barry instantly picked up on.

"Purposely vague, I like it! I have to say, the two of you seem to have clicked rather well. No complaints?"

"No, none at all," said Franny.

"Seems like a different time and place would have worked a charm for the two of you!" Barry winked.

"What I guess I'm saying is, of course, it's best when we all get on with each other, just as I'm sure everyone else who's been swapped feels about their new partner too," said Franny.

"Of course, and there seems to have been a lot of getting on, if you catch my drift?" said Barry, reaching across and nudging Franny.

"No?" smiled Franny meekly.

"Some might even say, being Mrs. Cresswell has been an upgrade, so to speak?"

"Michael has been a wonderful husband," answered Franny, finding no other way of putting it.

"And it's a wrap! Thank you so much, this has all been rather insightful," said Barry turning off the cameras.

"That's surprising," Franny smiled uncomfortably. "Will you want to interview Michael too, he'll be so much more articulate than I was?"

"No, no. He's not a teacher here, is he? My story will focus on you lot."

Franny parted ways from the reporter and drove back to Cresswell Cottage, for her final weekend with Michael. She was excited for the two days they still had left, but was beginning to dread leaving, afterwards. She was also unsettled by the feeling that in the exceedingly short interview she'd just had with the eccentric reporter, she'd just put her foot in her mouth, though it eluded her as to exactly how.

CHAPTER TWENTY

"Don't put your handbag down yet, we're eating out, tonight!" announced John Webb the second he saw Jody walk through the front door.

"And am I to expect that I'm paying?" Jody asked, cynically.

"Technically, what's mine is yours and yours is mine – as this is a marriage, my dear. So, I could just as easily take care of those monetary formalities." The old man's mood was elevated, with the hope that Jody Cresswell would soon be a problem of the past, as long as he played along with her paranoid little plan. He smiled, raising his eyebrows in delight. Jody shook her head but felt less irritable as soon as she saw Lucy make her way downstairs to join them.

"Who's driving?" asked Jody, looking to Lucy.

"I'm a very nervous provisional driver, I'm afraid. I only feel comfortable with mum in the car as she's giving me driving lessons," Lucy smiled.

"Shall we?" said John Webb, fiddling in one of the side-pockets of his briefcase to retrieve his jingle of keys.

"In that?" asked Jody, glancing at the small, scarcely fit-to-drive, box of brown metal that was parked crookedly to one side of the driveway.

"Mum's car, when she's here, is much more in keeping with this century," said Lucy, sounding like a tour guide. Jody couldn't help but smile.

"Come on, let's just take mine, then." Jody dug out the remote control for her stylish and compact crossover. "But at least be a gentleman and drive," she tossed the comparably high-tech looking gadget towards the old man who caught it and began examining the thing as if trying to decode it.

"Fancy," John Webb finally remarked, adding "However, I'm fairly sure that all this technology is just a trend, much like your pseudo-cigarette malarkey."

"Hmph," said Jody, pulling open the backdoor and getting inside.

"Where are we going, dad? Am I dressed okay?" asked Lucy, getting in with Jody at the back.

"Yes, we all look great."

"Where does your family normally like going to eat out?" asked Jody.

"We normally don't," said Lucy. "Ed and I like exploring new venues with mum but it's usually for breakfast or lunch. It doesn't really work for Ed and dad to go to a public place together," she whispered, in a kind and confiding tone.

"Why not?"

"My dad and my brother haven't seen eye-to-eye since I can remember."

"But your brother seems nice enough, the little I've met him?" asked Jody, getting interested.

"Oh, he is – he's the nicest big brother I could ask for.

He's always looked out for me and he loves our family very much but..."

"Your father can be, how can I say it?" interrupted Jody.

"Annoying?" suggested Lucy.

"Yes, actually very," said Jody, tentatively. Lucy nodded with utmost neutrality, taking no issue whatsoever with how her father was being described. John Webb drove on obliviously. He'd quickly decided to take advantage of the very symbol of modernism that he'd questioned moments ago and turned up the volume on the front speaker system. He gleefully bounced along to Heart radio's partial repeat of last week's U.K. top forty.

"I think even though my brother loves my dad, he finds it difficult to like him. They end up clashing a lot."

"Oh?" said Jody, realizing that was probably a good way to describe her own feelings for Michael.

"You don't have any children, do you?" asked Lucy.

"No. How do you know?" asked Jody, a little thrown.

"It was just a hunch. And, Ed and I met up with mum for lunch last weekend so I figured if you did, mum would have mentioned something – she loves children, always has."

"Oh. I do too, I guess we just never got around to it," said Jody, not wanting to get into the nitty-gritty.

"You might still be able to. Plus, you could adopt, even later on," said Lucy, in what seemed to Jody, a very naive way of seeing the world.

"Right." Jody took a deep breath and thought what she never said to anyone, not even Michael. That the reason she'd chosen not to have a baby wasn't because she couldn't stand the explosive nappies or the sleepless nights. It was because she'd been paralyzed by the fear that she wouldn't make a good mum.

For so many years, the notion that she was too selfish and cold, much like her own mother, had gnawed away any initial self-esteem she'd had for the undertaking of motherhood. And yet even for her own shortcomings that she was so brutally aware of, she'd known all along that Michael would have made a good father. And, had she just followed his lead, she too, could have softened enough to trust her own instincts. Trust, thought Jody, sounded so easy in theory and yet constantly deserted her when she needed it most. Even if she would have made a terrible mother, Michael, with all his sensitivities could have made up for both of them.

"I'm sure your mum did a stellar job of raising you two," said Jody looking at Lucy. Though she didn't let it surface, she felt an inward pang of jealousy that being nurturing came so easily to women like Franny.

"She's a wonderful mum. And I don't mean this badly against dad but mum has been like two parents to us most of our lives. We love dad for who he is but mum has always been there for us – no matter what."

Jody gave a brief nod in Lucy's direction and said nothing. And yet the penny finally dropped. Michael was like a male version of Franny and had they taken the path they'd both yearned to take, and had a family, the likelihood was that their children wouldn't have been messed up little delinquents. If a girl as sweet as Lucy could attribute half of her parentage to John Webb and still turn out the way she had, thanks to just one normal parent and her own resilience, then anything was possible. Even Ed seemed normal enough, thought Jody. And as far as not enjoying John Webb's company, for her that spoke more of Ed's sanity than it did of any deficit within him. The boy hadn't done badly at all. In fact, he'd thrived with that fly of an old man buzzing around his head constantly, for more than two decades – that was the hardiness of children. Jody's heart sank as it dawned heavy on her that perhaps she should have taken a chance with Michael and had the baby they'd always dreamed of.

"Sorry, I took the wrong street," said the old man as he approached the Westquay shopping centre carpark.

"Aren't we going to one of the restaurants there?" asked Jody.

"It appears we might be dining at the Premier Inn!" said Lucy, excitedly. Jody rolled her eyes in disparagement.

"All will be revealed in just a minute," said John Webb, driving past the Premier Inn. He proceeded to pull into the underground parking at Ikea.

"What's going on?" asked Jody firmly, as the old man went down one level and promptly pulled in, to a parking space that another car had been signalling to occupy.

"Follow me!" said John Webb, jumping out of the car and almost running towards the elevators.

"Should I get a trolley?" asked Lucy as if they were going for a regular round of furniture shopping.

"What would we need that for?" asked the old man as Jody and Lucy caught up to him in the empty elevator.

"Look, I'm not really sure what's going on here but I'm getting hungry," said Jody.

"Ta-da!" said John Webb stepping out of the elevator and running ahead into the cafeteria.

"Oh dear," said Lucy, trying to brace for Jody's reaction.

"What the heck? Is he seriously suggesting we eat here?" asked Jody too flabbergasted to say anything more vicious.

John Webb fetched a couple of trays and ushered them into the line-up, feeling proud. "This place is awesome! You can pick up an extra rug or two and feed your starving family!"

"I – I – this is, why would anyone want to eat here by choice?" said Jody, gazing at the pictures of food up ahead.

"Swedish meatballs!" said John Webb licking his lips.

"Mystery meat," replied Jody shaking her head.

"They're actually not bad at all," said Lucy, amused.

As they paid and found some limited seating in the corner of the cafeteria with their meals, Jody prodded at the contents of her plate, with her fork.

"You've never been here, have you?" asked Lucy cutting into one of her meatballs and dipping it into a splodge of lingonberry sauce.

"What do you think?" said Jody sulkily. "We don't even shop here. Quite honestly, when I think of this place, I only think of a first-year university student, who has few if any food options because they're up to their eyeballs in loans."

"Try some, you might enjoy it," urged Lucy as if she was negotiating with a fussy five-year-old.

"Do you like it?"

"Oh yes, when we were growing up, we actually used to come here every Sunday for lunch. I think it was mum's idea to come here once to buy some whisks and kitchen utensils because she was really into baking."

"I bet," scoffed Jody.

"We came back here the following Sunday to get a few more items and it just sort of stuck," Lucy smiled.

Jody said nothing but instead, closed her eyes and took a small bite of her meatball. She was pleasantly surprised by the taste and texture. She begrudgingly found herself drawing parallels with a gourmet restaurant that she'd visited with some friends, a month ago.

"What do you think?" asked Lucy. John Webb licked

his stealthily polished off plate and stared expectantly at Jody's food.

"It's okay," admitted Jody.

"If you can't finish it, I can always help you?" asked the old man.

"That won't be necessary." Jody tucked in, not wanting to give the old man an assumed opening. She finished every morsel and was hugely irritated by the way John Webb continued to watch her every bite.

"Do you ever bring Franny on dates or surprise dinners out?" asked Jody.

"We're married, isn't that more something young people do?"

"You are joking, I hope?" asked Jody, lowering her voice.

"Well we're a seasoned couple. Despite what you think about Michael, Franny is crazy about me. She doesn't need posh dinners to continue feeling the love that I inspire each day."

"How are you so cocky? What makes you think she even loves you? Sorry Lucy, no offence."

Lucy stared from Jody to her father, as interested as Jody, in the answers to the questions. Until recently, it hadn't really occurred to her to think about her parents' relationship. Her father's peculiar contributions had been a given. And unlike Ed, Lucy had found something strangely comforting about his antics – like the white noise of a television or the radio playing in the background. Despite living in the midst of it, until Jody Cresswell's arrival in their home, it hadn't struck Lucy that marriages like Franny's were tough arrangements that taught the virtue of patience but gave little else in return. Having always been partial to literary romances, Lucy had just assumed that she'd eventually meet someone handsome, charming and considerate, who'd whisk her off her feet.

And now, though it had taken her a so much of her life to get there, she was starting to see that the things Jody had taken strong exception to, were in fact important. Everyone deserved to feel as loved as the love they gave and Lucy had started, in her own gentle way, to question whether her father was in fact the best choice for her mother. She wondered how her mum felt about the matter and whether she'd ever given it any thought. From the discontent that had surfaced following her parents' anniversary earlier that year, Lucy supposed she had.

"It's okay," Lucy said to Jody. "Actually dad, every now and then, I wonder the same thing. How do you know mum is happy with you?"

"Trust me, when you're married to the person, it's something you just know." The old man scratched his head and peered around slightly confused, like he was trying to decide if what he'd said was true. He checked his watch and scanned the bustling canteen. "I think we still have a couple of moments. Can I get you ladies anything else?"

"Couple of moments for what? Is there some kind of eating schedule where we have to vacate our seats after twenty or thirty minutes?" Jody too began looking around the room, trying to find signage posted on the wall.

"No, dear woman, nothing of the sort. I've taken the initiative of arranging our second interview right here!" said John Webb merrily.

"You mean with that awful reporter?"

"Exactly. He quibbled a bit, something about wanting to use the house again but I insisted he'd get a better picture right here, at our family meal out." John Webb made his way back into the queue. He searched the chilled shelf for the largest piece of Daim cake he could find and grabbed an empty mug for some coffee.

"What should I do? I don't think I want to be interviewed too," said Lucy sounding nervous.

"And I don't think you should have to. Do you want to take a quick look around and just keep your distance until everything's over?" asked Jody, wanting both, to ease Lucy's discomfort but secretly, also wanting to be able to talk openly about Franny because it wouldn't necessarily be good. What Lucy thought, had begun to matter.

"Yes please," said Lucy, quickly standing to take her leave.

"There you are, hidden in plain sight!" said Barry McGuinty, approaching Jody. He appeared quite mismatched with his surroundings, wearing dark aviators indoors, in the evening, paired with cream corduroys.

"Hi," said Jody, briefly shaking hands.

"I really wanted this second scene shot at the Webb home but your current hubby suggested that this location would be just what this wife swap needed most of all. Now I wish I'd asked him to elaborate on such a vague statement. Oh well, where is he?"

"Getting ready to stuff his face with round two of the world's most mass-produced and sloppily assembled food," replied Jody, pointing at the line-up where the old man was paying for his cake and coffee.

"Ah," said Barry, setting up his equipment and fiddling with one of the lenses.

"Evening all!" chirped John Webb, sitting back down with his fare.

"Evening, sir!" replied Barry with a bemused look. "When we spoke last week, the two of you were so far off the page with each other, that you weren't even reading from the same book. How have things progressed since then?" The reporter watched with his mouth almost watering as John Webb took a big bite of his solid, chocolate-covered cake.

"We're sitting in the middle of an Ikea, having eaten the most generic meal of my adult life, Barry – that is how things have progressed."

"I take it you've been shopping?" asked Barry.

"No, actually I decided to treat us all to a nice family meal out." The old man beamed as he slurped his coffee.

"Wait a minute, you came here just to eat a meal?" asked Barry doing a double-take.

"Yes, and this has been the most satisfying meal I've had in almost two weeks – and surely that says everything," complained Jody.

"Well, yes. It says a lot."

"And what it says, is that I'm a kind and generous soul who knows what his family, specifically his wife wants and needs."

"That's not what it says at all!" snapped Jody.

"What does it say?" asked Barry, zooming in on Jody's face.

It says that before this wife swap, I took my sweet, kind, generous husband for granted for far too long. Because there are men like him in his world." Jody gestured towards John Webb. "And now...I fear it's all too late."

"Again, strong words from a flailing wife. And why do you feel like that, Jody?"

"Because I've been keeping an eye on Franny Webb at school – and her husband here, has been helping me. And what we've seen, is the face of a woman desperately in love with a better life. And, I'm so scared that my poor, gullible husband will fall for her sultry charms.

"So really, this is my appeal to you Michael – please wait for me, your wife with whom you took vows that promised forever!"

"Powerful stuff!" said Barry appearing exceedingly moved. "And John, would you like to say a few words?"

"All I'll say is, Franny, my love, we're married – have been for half of our lives. You're the love of my life and being around Jody has really shown me what it would be like, if I were ever to lose you. Please. Come. Home." John Webb could have been mistaken as someone whose wife was missing without a trace, rather than swapped.

"Touching," said Jody, "even an appeal for his wife, is really an appeal for him."

"You're a good woman, sweet-pea and you make my life better by being in it," the old man proceeded. "Recently, I've realized just how much I've taken you for granted and if you give me one more chance, I'll make it up to you. I know now that you wanted to go to Paris and not Prague for our anniversary.

"If you come back to me after this dreadfully thorny period in our lives is over, I'll take you to Paris – for real! In fact, I promise you, that in the next ten minutes, I'm going to go ahead and book the tickets in anticipation that we will make this happen – for I'm a dreamer and I believe in us." John Webb wore his signature look, which was a hybrid of pathetic and loveable pet dog.

"And here we have it folks, laid bare before us, the dark side of wife swap, where these two innocent teachers have had their lives ripped apart by something as seemingly innocent as a fundraiser, to get sponsored upgrades for Summerfield Community School. I'm Barry McGuinty, thank you.

CHAPTER TWENTY-ONE

Franny felt as though the past two weeks had been an exotic vacation abroad and now the moment was speedily drawing near, when she'd have to return to her mundane old life, like it had all been a dream. She imagined that living with Michael felt in some way as special as she'd feel if she were visiting Paris. Saturday had been an easy day where they'd both chosen to ignore the impending end of their current situation.

They'd taken a walk along the edge of the water at Gunwharf Quays and then gone to Brasserie Blanc for a long and late lunch that had eventually turned into an early dinner by the time they'd polished off their bottle of bubbles. Franny had never had so much fun in her entire life. At least Lucy was coming to the age where Franny could envision them going for a spot of shopping followed by such gastronomic adventures in the coming years. But like every mum, Franny hoped that though her relationship with her daughter would continue to grow closer, there would come a stage when Lucy too would spread her wings and fly the nest. She wished for a future when her daughter would want to meet up despite having a full and satisfying life of her own, instead of because she didn't. Franny also wished that she'd made more friends since settling down and having a family. But frankly, maintaining friendships had proved hard when she'd had no one to look after Ed and Lucy when they were too young to stay home alone. The old man had always been too infinitely distractible to be trusted when faced with the antics of young children. As the children had grown, Franny had tried hosting a book club, as well as various attempts at wine and cheese evenings with her artsy friends from university. Sadly, even these had been disasters as soon as John Webb had announced his presence with some or the other noisy hobby or just his incessant and unwelcome whining when he'd imposed himself on the group of women and taken a seat next to Franny and stayed for the whole evening. His attendance at every such get-together had put off enough of her friends, that fewer and fewer of them would show up at each gathering. Eventually, they'd stopped inviting her over at all, knowing that she'd want to reciprocate and host at her house again.

The day had ended with watching a travel documentary on Netflix that involved exploring different cultures from all over the world. Franny had been intrigued to learn that apart from France, Michael had also spent a gap year during university, backpacking around Australia and more recently (just before marrying Jody), he'd been to Brazil and Goa. Since being with Jody, he'd holidayed consistently to Nice in the summer and the Lake District in the spring. Michael had managed to convince Jody to do a few long weekends wondering around Christmas markets in Europe over the years but Franny identified that his globe-trotting streak was still itching to find expression.

Sunday unfolded with a wholly different tone. The day had started with Franny going downstairs to the smell of fresh coffee and chocolate croissants baking in the ample oven. However, a tension hung between them as they both pondered who'd be the first to raise the dreaded topic of Franny's looming departure, less than twenty-four hours away.

"It's been just wonderful, being here with you," said Franny taking a sip of coffee and breaking a croissant in half, watching the chocolate lazily trickle onto her plate.

"You can say that again," Michael sighed as he watched Franny from across the table.

"These are scrumptious by the way."

"I think two months, no two years, wouldn't even have been enough for me. Actually, no amount of months, or even years, would ever feel enough with someone like you," he said taking Franny's hand. "One day these couple of weeks are going to be like a flash in the pan." Michael was sullen. He seemed younger than his forty-three years and yet also a lot older.

"They'll never be a flash in the pan for me," said Franny, squeezing his hand. "If I'm to be truthful, I don't think I've ever enjoyed myself so much and indulged like this. I'll never forget you."

They ate their breakfast mostly in silence, intermittently trying to make jokes and start a conversation but unlike the days that lay behind them, words kept stalling. Afterwards, Franny went upstairs and started packing up her belongings. In just a fortnight, she'd become comfortable in a place that she never could've guessed would even tolerate her presence let alone nurture it the way it had. Franny looked about the place and no longer saw Cresswell Cottage as Jody's house, only a beautiful space that had allowed her and Michael to discover parts of themselves that had been hidden away for so long. Franny was unnerved as she mused upon whether her own home would in some way, feel strange to her upon her return.

"I just got a text from Jody, instructing me to watch the BBC story about the wife swap. She's also specifically asked that I tell you to tune in," said Michael coming into the room and looking all the worse for seeing Franny's packed suitcase.

"Right, of course, when is it airing?" asked Franny, growing more uneasy than she'd been before.

"In five minutes – typical Jody, what if we'd been out?"

"To be fair, I probably should have had some inkling about the slot. I think I was just trying to ignore it because I'm so nervous about seeing myself on television," said Franny, as they made their way to the living room. Michael grabbed the remote as they both sat down to watch.

"Good afternoon! On this week's show about what's new and trending in our communities across England, we're featuring a school in the south that's raising money in a way that's unique. Summerfield Community School is set to be getting some rather handsome funding grants from interested partners," said the voice of an attractive woman at the news desk. Franny felt her stomach churn and Michael winked, attempting to ease her discontent.

"Mr. Flounders, the headteacher at Summerfield Community School, thought up the idea of asking his staff to take part in a wife swap, where each teacher involved, is being sponsored for some pretty major improvements and upgrades to equipment for their department.

"The wife swap concludes tomorrow after school and our resident correspondent, Barry McGuinty, has been getting to know everyone involved over the past two weeks.

"Barry took an in-depth look at what life during such an unprecedented event was like. Now, over to Barry." There was a close-up shot of the presenter, who probably moonlighted as a model for a toothpaste advert when she wasn't hosting the news. She smiled broadly before the camera.

The scene then cut to more familiar scenes of the school. First up was Mr. Flounders, chin-up and looking pleased as he explained the wife swap in great depth, including all the new renovations the school would undergo. He thanked the staff for being gracious and talked of Natalie Stone's sophisticated methods by which she'd matched each staff member for an optimal experience.

Next came snippets of interviews from various colleagues stationed in different rooms in the school. Franny smiled when Emma was shown in her music class, amidst students, saying that it had been quite an experience. She wore an amused expression that said it all. Eva Batchford came on immediately afterwards, declaring how it had been too long and although it was a worthwhile event to have partaken in, she missed her own husband. She complained that though he'd looked after her well enough, Emma Blue's spouse wasn't her cup of tea. Franny found it highly cheeky and a bit ironic that Eva had eluded to Charlie Blue being a dry and boring partner.

Then, Franny suddenly saw the inside of her living room splash onto the screen and Barry's voice could be heard though his face couldn't be seen.

"Unfortunately, not everyone found themselves taken care of during this wife swap. There were members of staff who were saddled with the wretched unions of their colleagues and as a result, unearthed the underlying threat to their own unsuspecting marriages."

The camera rolled on as Jody ranted and raved about

John Webb's inadequacies as well as Franny's so-called designs to seek out an upgrade to her life in the arms of Michael Cresswell. Then, as Barry followed a piercing sound up the stairs, to reveal John Webb blowing his whistles in full-swing in the thread-bare guest bedroom, more condemnation followed.

"Oh dear," Franny groaned but that was just the beginning of what had turned from a simple coverage into an exposé. Next came Franny's interview. Staring at the screen mortified, she quickly determined what an utter twat she came across as. The clip showed her nodding along and grinning like a Cheshire cat about how she had found Michael to be a wonderful husband. The last piece was chaotic and was neither of the school and nor of the Webb residence.

"Why did he take them to Ikea?" asked Michael, trying to keep a composed demeanour in the face of the bitter accusations his wife hurled at Franny.

Franny said nothing but one hand went up to cover her mouth as Jody and then John Webb, made desperate appeals on television, for her and Michael to refrain from walking out on them, after their torrid affair.

Barry McGuinty concluded the segment by highlighting the dark and potentially unethical side of the hedonistic headteacher's little experiment. Mr Flounders was heavily implicated as the greedy, power-mad figure who'd do anything for some fame and fortune.

"Bastard," announced Franny in a small but meaningful voice, unable to tear her eyes away from the flat screen. Michael wasn't sure whether she meant Barry, John Webb or Mr. Flounders.

"I don't know where to begin or even what to say," was all Michael managed.

"Am I really that appalling?" asked Franny, turning her gaze towards her lap.

"No! God, no!" said Michael, coming to lean down next to Franny. "It's not you, none of this!"

"You heard Jody, she wouldn't have said all those things, nonetheless on national television, if she didn't think they were true.

"Oh dear, I should have given her more reassurances – she came to me to complain about John and how she wasn't happy with him. And then, I detected that in the last few days, she'd become the target of chitchatting mouths. I should have seen this coming," Franny lamented.

"You listen to me, Franny Webb," said Michael taking Franny's hands in his, "there is nothing you should have done differently.

"Jody is the world's biggest tattler. And, on this occasion she got on the wrong end of her own, useless pursuit because she acted like a drama queen about her so-called hardship with John – none of this is about you, or even me.

"It's about two people who appear to have met their match and realized how ruddy hard they are to live with, do you hear me?"

"But she feels that I've ruined her marriage," said Franny. She burst into tears of frustration that were so very long in the making. She wept, not just for all the cruel accusations Jody had made but because she felt embarrassed that some of them were probably even true.

"You haven't ruined anything! Getting to know me, you must have gathered that we've been having problems for almost our entire marriage. That's about seven years of anguish and heartache for both of us in our own ways."

"But maybe if this wife swap hadn't happened, you would have worked things out. Or maybe, we should have kept our distance and not enjoyed each other's company so much?"

"You can't live life by avoiding what makes you happy because your happiness may not sit right with another person," said Michael, smiling a little. "You've taught me that."

"I never thought about things that way," said Franny wiping away a tear.

"I have a feeling, we've both been living hollow lives for ages because it never occurred to us to rock the boat. We were too busy attending to whims to even think about what made our day a little more special."

"You're not wrong there – more often than not, John doesn't even know I'm there and it's not because we're so comfortable with each other. It's because he's oblivious to anyone that isn't him." Franny blew her nose, feeling better. "But how will I face everyone tomorrow at school?" she moaned, searching Michael's eyes for an answer.

"With all the gusto that you have inside of you – you kind, courageous woman! Because who cares what anyone else thinks?" Michael beamed.

"Is it really that easy?"

"If you let it be, it is. And do you want to know how I know this?" asked Michael. Franny nodded enthusiastically. "Because being around you has opened me up to greater possibilities for my life. I don't want to waste another moment, running around pleasing everyone apart from myself.

"This past little while, I've learnt what it's like to breathe deeply, like I really mean it and not run around trying to meet impossible standards and still falling short. You've let me be me and that's the most amazing gift someone can give to another person. And we make a great team."

"That we do," agreed Franny, feeling that as long as she kept staring into those deep oceanic eyes, she'd feel no fear of the day ahead, nor any regrets from her past.

"I want to propose something, if you'd indulge me?" said Michael after a pause.

"Of course."

"I've already made my decision – I want to start afresh. And I'd like to do it with you."

"This is all so much to take in," said Franny, feeling like what she'd watched play out for all to hear and see on TV just a short few minutes ago, now paled in comparison to Michael's revelation.

"It's okay, there's no rush. Take all the time you need," said Michael settling back onto the seat next to her.

"I honestly didn't think you liked me like that."

"I thought I made it pretty obvious," Michael laughed. "Why, how do *you* like me? I'm sorry if I've grossly overstepped – maybe you don't feel for me what I do for you."

"I'm so attracted to you," said Franny, strangely relieved to be saying it out in the open "...both inside and out".

"Wait here, I need to get something," Michael suddenly arose from the sofa. He came right back, with a gift bag.

"Oh Michael, what is it? You didn't need to do this!" said Franny.

"It wasn't just me, you did it too. Let's take a look inside, shall we?" Michael gave the bag to Franny. She opened it and out came the two mugs that they'd crafted together in their first ever pottery class a week ago. Michael had had them glazed a rich, jade tone.

"Yours is amazing," said Franny, blushing as to how

misshapen hers was by comparison, though less than she remembered.

"I made it for you."

"Michael! Are you sure?"

"If you don't believe me, check what I carved into the bottom of mine when you were busy making yours."

"Franny, from my heart to yours, Michael," Franny read the inscription.

"It's the most beautiful present I've ever received that wasn't from Ed and Lucy," said Franny giddily.

"I'll take that as a very high compliment!"

"I mean it as one," Franny took the mug and held it, "I'll treasure this so much. And, I want you to have mine but it might not be worth treasuring – look at how mangled it is." Franny laughed.

"It's something you made and I saw how hard you worked at it, that makes it something I'll cherish. Every morning when I drink from it, I'll think about you."

"That's very kind of you. I'll think about you too.

Isn't it funny that I'm an art teacher and my mug is so sloppy?"

"It's always the way. If it makes you feel better, I'm a policeman who can't for his life, solve those whodunnit murder mystery games they play at dinner parties."

"I'm sure you're very good at your job!"

"As I am, that you're good at yours."

"Did you by any chance see those artistic posters on the wall to the side of me in Townsend Hall in the interview? They were done by my students for the musical tomorrow night."

"Well at least there's an up-side to that hideously sub-standard interview," said Michael. They both burst into laughter, shaking their heads.

"It'll blow over, eventually, right?" asked Franny, breathing out a sigh.

"A hundred percent. And by the way, I am serious about what I said. I have feelings for you – and if you'd like to consider a life different to the one you've been leading, then I hope we can see a lot more of each other, rather than less after tomorrow."

"Michael, I feel exactly the same way about you, gosh, I can't even believe I'm actually saying this! Let me think about things?"

"I've never met anyone like you. And, no matter what you decide, this was the best risk I've ever taken," said Michael as they went in for a kiss.

CHAPTER TWENTY-TWO

Monday morning was abuzz with the fallout of the interview clip from the previous day. Franny went straight to her classroom before school began and her absence was quickly noted by Emma who came looking for her.

"Room service!" said Emma cheerfully. She opened the door and knocked before coming inside.

"That's very sweet of you," said Franny self-consciously.

"Didn't feel like coming out to see us, today?"

"Considering the circumstances, I thought it might be better to stay away, at least until we're all back and settled."

"None of what happened was your fault, Fran. And if I may say, Jody made her own bed. I mean there isn't one of us in that staffroom who hadn't been talking her down from her bitching for the past two weeks!"

"That interview just brought everything out into the open though, didn't it?" said Franny, trying to find some solace in her steaming cup of coffee.

"That was all on Jody."

"And John."

"Yes, John likely didn't help matters. But living with that woman, she probably got into his head and insisted he bolster her message. Things will die down when she goes back to her self-masochistic husband tonight and comes back gloating tomorrow, about the rose-petals he had strewn all over the house for her."

"He's leaving her," said Franny, flatly.

"No! Really?"

"He told me in very clear terms that it's over."

"I knew she was feeling wildly threatened by the set-up and sure, it came across that it was probably because they had existing issues but still, I'm shocked!"

"And what's worse, I feel I'm to blame."

"Why? I've said it before, have you met Jody Cresswell? Can you even begin to fathom what it must be like to live with such an unhappy person?"

"Actually, I can. Michael talked about it very frankly. But that's not all..." Franny wished Emma could read minds.

"What else?" asked Emma.

"Michael has feelings for me. If I choose to leave John, he wants to give things a try with us. Of course, there's no pressure or anything from his side. And... we kissed."

"Woah! That's big! How do you feel about all this?"

"I'm delighted by Michael. He's kind, considerate, witty and so handsome. I didn't know men like him even existed – at least not for someone like me."

"Someone like you? What, with your two heads and being covered in scales from head to toe? What are you talking about? Men like Michael should be with women like you."

"You're only saying that because you don't like Jody."

"No, I'm saying it because I care about you and think

you deserve some happiness. Don't get me wrong, if you choose to stay with John, I'm always here for you. But, if you do think there is another road you want to take, then – again as your friend, I'm very much here for you."

"Thank you," said Franny.

"And don't give a stuff what anyone else says, they don't know what happens behind closed doors, though in your case, they might have a pretty good guess."

"I have a decision I'm leaning towards and I think I'll know what I have to do by the end of today. How about you? You must be so excited to be going back home to Charlie?"

"I am, with bells on! And you know what? Before coming to find you, I just got a phone call from him. He asked me if I could book some vacation for the rest of the week as he's whisking me off to Champneys health spa as a pick-me-up from all the madness."

"That sounds like the perfect end to a very boring fortnight," smiled Franny. "Did you and Eva manage to patch things up?"

"I'm happy to say, we ran into each other in the staffroom and cleared the air before tonight's performance."

"Thank heavens! What did she say?"

"She was in a very good mood! I think she said all that stuff about Charlie because underneath everything, she really missed her husband. And, just because he wasn't all chummy with me, doesn't mean they aren't a well-suited couple. I think they might both be introverts who need their space. I guess they instinctively seek to give that to each other."

"I'm very glad to hear that. But didn't she say Charlie was the quiet one?"

"I think some people just project their own insecurities onto the other person. Look at Jody."

"Do you think Mr. Flounders will let you go away at such short notice?" asked Franny.

"Ah, I think he will – after all, our headmaster is the one who should bear the brunt for his zany scheme and all the, ahem, trauma it's caused his staff."

"Agreed," said Franny, "although I have him to thank too, his fundraiser has made me see things in a way I never would have otherwise. I've always accepted my fate, that things will never change for me. It's been a stable but predictable life and it never dawned on me until meeting Michael, that it could be more."

"Keep your chin up – it'll all work out the way it's supposed to," said Emma, hugging her friend and getting up to make her way to her own classroom.

CHAPTER TWENTY-THREE

The entire staff and almost all of the school had turned up to the debut performance of *Grease*. Franny and Emma entered Townsend Hall together so they could sit in a special area dedicated to teachers who'd helped and the parents of those who were performing in the musical.

"Look, there's John!" said Emma pointing to Franny's old man across the gangway, "is he wearing a bow-tie?"

"I think he is!" said Franny, squinting to get a better look. John Webb waved at them as he'd been looking to catch Franny's attention. He then started gesturing at Franny with his little finger and thumb sticking out towards his ear and mouth.

"Does he want you to call him?" asked Emma.

"I'm not sure," replied Franny gesturing back to try and communicate that she couldn't understand. She pointed to the doors, trying to say that they could go outside and chat during the intermission. The old man nodded vigorously.

Jody Cresswell watched the pair of them as they talked across to each other and felt like she could have punched them both in their smug little faces. She instantly knew that

Franny had been eluding her all day by avoiding any communal spaces and the thought to storm her classroom had crossed her mind frequently throughout the day. She decided there and then that she'd have it out with the unassuming woman who had turned into her direct rival, before the night was out.

A very sheepish looking Mr. Flounders opened the very first show with a dramatic speech about the sheer talent of the cast and those helping behind the scenes. Franny's stomach lurched as she caught Jody staring at her with daggers, sitting one row across from John Webb.

The lights began to dim and the show opened to energetic cheers as the theme of *Grease* came on. Emma clapped along enthusiastically to the beat and soon, the rest of the audience had joined in. Franny got a high from seeing her friend so happy. Emma nodded her head, keeping in rhythm with the music, instinctively making sure the tempo and choreography were on track. Franny thought the show ran smoother than it ever had before and if there were any minor errors in timing or dialogue, she couldn't tell. Every now and then as the lights changed, Franny would catch a glimpse of Jody watching her as intently as everyone else was watching the stage. She looked for Eva who was most likely back-stage, prepping her students as they came on. Franny had no doubt that Eva must have known every line by heart and was keenly hanging on it, silently mouthing along as Sandy and Danny sauntered around on stage, surrounded by their loyal Pink Ladies and T-Birds. She too felt a wave of excitement watching the students, who were no longer teenaged attendees of Summerfield Community School but transformed by the power of artistic expression, into the rebels of Rydell High, set so many decades ago and, a whole continent away.

The intermission came straight after "Greased Lightnin'" and Emma reported back to Eva, that judging by the crackle in the audience, how well-received the performance had been so far. Mr. Flounders, who would normally have been working the crowd to a point where he may as well have done a number by himself in sequins on stage, was nowhere to be seen after introducing the show.

"He was 'ere, sitting a couple of rows down from me, but he legged it just before the break. I think the bloke wanted to dodge all the questions from parents who saw the wife swap fiasco yesterday," Darren Easy filled in Eva and Emma, pleased at being the chief discloser of gossip now that Jody had been ousted.

"Probably a good move, tonight's about the children – the real stars of our school," said Emma. Eva nodded, brimming with pride and the euphoria that comes from heartily nurturing potential, and it paying off.

"I was hoping I could talk to you, my dear," said John Webb, coming up to Franny.

"Of course, should we go somewhere quieter?" asked Franny, finding unexpected comfort in seeing her husband properly after so many days.

"Yes, let's step outside for some fresh air?"

They slowly clambered out of the main hall, past the public area and outside into the evening air that had taken on a cool effervescence, thanks to a rain shower that appeared to have just ended. John Webb sullied the crisp freshness by swiftly lighting up a cigarette and taking a deep drag.

"Did you see the news yesterday?" asked the old man, expectantly.

"Yes," said Franny, hoping that wasn't the extent of their conversation.

"So...?"

"So, what, John?" asked Franny, a little annoyed.

"Would you like to go to Paris with me?"

"It depends – would you like to go?"

"Yes," said the old man.

"Then answer me one question: in all these years, why didn't we?"

"I don't know, I guess life got in the way. And you know what it's like raising kids – they're like little bloodsuckers. They suck away at life, energy, money," John Webb winked and his eyes twinkled like he'd made a colossally witty remark.

"Ed and Lucy are the ones who have suggested we take the trip, for several years now," said Franny, unamused.

"Err, right. Any-who, we can go now – it's never too late, is it?"

"Okay, if you genuinely want to do it, be honest, have you booked the tickets for us?"

"Aye?" John Webb puffed away at the last of his cigarette and squished it into the wet ground.

"On the interview, you said that basically the minute you were off screen, you were going to go ahead and book our tickets, just in the hope that I'd go with you. So I take it, true to word, you must already have done the due preparations. That if I say yes, we're all set and ready to go?" Where Franny would normally have been nervous, she felt only solid determination. Once and for all, she wanted to know if her husband was capable of change.

"Well, you'll be pleased to know,"

"Yes?" she asked, a glint of optimism rising within.

"That, I almost booked them yesterday – only I couldn't because when we got back from the restaurant, I remembered Ed's not been home and I didn't have use of his laptop. You know me, all I have is my old typewriter, which isn't hooked up to the world wide web."

"And you didn't think to ask Lucy for hers?"

"Well, no, I got quite distracted as Jody began making a racket by packing her things away. Besides, I didn't really think you'd mind when we booked them as long as we did at some point in the near future."

"Okay, John. It's good to know," replied Franny, suddenly gaining all the clarity she needed to help her make a decision about her future.

"There you are!" said Jody Cresswell, as Franny and John Webb walked through the main doors to go back inside for the remainder of the performance.

Franny quickly twigged by the frantic look on Jody's face, that she been looking for her since the start of intermission. Franny smiled, wanting to stay as polite as possible. She braced herself for an ambush. She saw that a crowd of interested teachers and even some parents had immediately formed around them.

"Hi, Jody," she said demurely.

"Hi. Don't worry, I just want to talk to you," said Jody, sounding surprisingly respectful.

"Okay. How are you?"

"I'm okay. I know we need to go back in, in the next couple of minutes but could we nip to the ladies, for some privacy?"

"Sure." Franny followed Jody as she moved through the crowd, with the same authority that she always did. They went across to the other side of the building, where it was virtually deserted.

"Look, I know I was tough on you in that interview."

"Yes, you were," said Franny, for once not apologizing for the other person's misdemeanour.

"I've always cared about what others thought of me. And this stupid wife swap has been my undoing at the school. I'm the one who talks about people and now, I'm the one who's the hot topic of gossip."

"You must know, that's your doing? I haven't, to my knowledge, said or done anything that would make people talk about us," said Franny, gently holding her own.

"I just felt so insecure about you and Michael."

"Why?"

"Because every day since that first evening, you came to school glowing. I've never seen you look that way before. And then, being at your home, with your husband made me realize what your regular life must be like."

"Yes, you certainly brought that across yesterday," said Franny remembering some of the awful things that had been said.

"I know. And I'm very sorry. Being away has made me realize how much I love Michael. And that we had a rocky relationship long before you and I were swapped. I just ignored things in the vain hope that everything would just magically be okay, one day."

"You don't need to worry about there being a Michael and I," said Franny, knowing at that point, just how devasting it would be for Jody if she pursued a relationship or even a friendship with Michael Cresswell.

Jody perked up straightaway, glancing in the mirrors opposite and preening her hair, with a grin. Franny flinched, in pain for herself, that she wouldn't be seeing Michael again and with a pang of empathy for Jody who had yet to learn that her marriage was over.

The bell rang to indicate the end of intermission and the two of them walked over to the main hall, together. Franny was silent, though Jody chattered on excitedly about the twists and turns, what had started out as an insipid fundraiser, had taken.

"Can we finish our chat after the show is over?" asked Franny, knowing that she couldn't let Jody go home and be blindsided by what awaited her.

"Yes, I'd love that – meet you outside!" said Jody strolling through the entrance to Townsend Hall and blowing a kiss in the air at Franny as she disappeared into the darkness of the already dimmed hall.

"Did I just see you and Queen Cresswell walk in together? More importantly, what did John have to say for himself?" asked Emma in a hushed voice as Franny took her seat next to her.

"Yes, you did and John and I had one of our usual chats," replied Franny.

"Oh?", said Emma as the music began and everyone clapped along to the short introduction as the actors skipped back onto the stage, ready for the next song.

"It's Raining on Prom Night", blared out of a big juke box that had been hired especially for the night and as the music faded to make room for the dialogue, Franny second guessed whether it was her place to give Jody the inside scoop on something as personal as her marriage.

She imagined what it would feel like for someone who was little more than an acquaintance come up to her and tell her things about her life that were none of their business. But then again, Franny had already had her home and relationship splashed across national television, not once but twice as she'd learned that the same segment had aired again during the evening news. She felt no spite towards Jody – in some ways, her brash and rather accusatory statement had proved to bring some objectivity into the situation. Franny had had a glimpse into what had essentially been her own life for so many years.

And what if Michael had changed his mind? What if his declaration had been nothing more than his way of venting his frustration – something Franny could closely relate to? What if Jody went home and was met with, as Emma had predicted, rose petals everywhere and maybe even a bottle of champagne to accompany a heartfelt and beautifully, homecooked meal? Franny grappled with her dilemma for the rest of the second act and it was only as the audience arose from their seats, applauding and waving at the cast for a job well done, that Franny's gut instinct prevailed and answered her question for her.

"Hello!" Jody caught hold of Franny's arm so they wouldn't lose each other in the sea of people that had washed into the area outside the hall, after the show had concluded.

"Hi," smiled Franny, "gosh it's really busy here isn't it? Why don't we talk in my car, it's parked quite close to the entrance?" She waved goodbye to Emma who was stuck in deep conversation with Eva and a couple of the parents.

"Yes, good thinking," replied Jody, looking around.

They strolled to the car and got in. Franny found the space a great relief after having been jammed against so many bodies, only moments earlier.

"Wasn't that an amazing performance?"

"Absolutely," said Franny, turning on the lights above them, so they could see each other a bit better than under the distant glow emanating from the security lights of Townsend Hall that hardly reached them under the cover of an old tree where the car was parked.

"Your art was fantastic, very professional."

Franny smiled, "Jody," she began.

"Can I make a confession?" Jody cut her off.

"Go ahead."

"I can't believe I'm about to say this but..." Jody exhaled, "John is a lot like me."

"How?" asked Franny, unable to see any likeness between the two.

"Even though your husband can be a bumbling fool who just can't get it right, I really do think that he loves you very much. He just doesn't know how to show it – something I'm guilty of myself with Michael."

"Showing it is as important as feeling it," said Franny.

"And I know that now. But honestly, despite going off at John throughout, I've gained insight into how he doesn't appear to ever have learnt how to survive in the world, alone. Much like me."

"Oh, Jody," sympathized Franny, recognising the truth in what she said.

"John and I need people like you and Michael in our lives more than anyone else. We're like the awkward kids in school who rely on our more mature and down-to-earth peers to befriend us." In that moment Jody was no longer the domineering and pompous tattler that she'd sculpted her reputation into but instead, a friendless and vulnerable girl, who like most others, had no real idea of what she was doing.

Franny teared up and knew that she needed to be honest. She sniffed away her own sadness and placed her hand on Jody's shoulder.

"I'm so sorry. I'm not sure what the future holds for you and Michael but yesterday he shared with me, that he...he felt he needed to move on."

"Hmm," said Jody, as the message sunk in.

"I didn't know whether it was for me to say anything but I couldn't let you go home without an inkling of what might be coming."

"I guess it shouldn't surprise me," said Jody after a few minutes in the stillness.

"I'm sure there's a chance he'll change his mind, once the two of you have talked things through?" consoled Franny, hoping for Jody's sake, that it could be true.

"No, if I know one thing about Michael, it's that he's a man of his word. If he decides something, there's no going back from it. He doesn't take matters of the heart, lightly."

"I'm very sorry."

"It's fine, really," said Jody putting on her game face, once more.

"But it always hurts, doesn't it? For the person making the decision as much as for the one hearing it."

"You know, underneath it all, I admire you. You have integrity and courage. John's a lucky man to have you. Do you think you'll be able to forgive him his wrongdoings?"

"I already have. Having said that, I've put John, his needs and wants first, my whole adult life."

"What are you saying?" asked Jody, with utmost sincerity and for once, no aim to extract gossip for curious ears.

"That it's time I think about myself and find what makes me feel most alive. And, that's no longer a marriage where I'm unseen and unheard." They hugged and Franny reached into her handbag retrieving a pack of travel-sized Kleenex tissues that she handed to Jody. "Take care of yourself and if you ever need a friend, I'm here," she said.

Franny switched off the lights and sat in the cool silence, contemplating the enormity of her own decision. As she watched cars roll out of the carpark, until hers was the only one that remained, a smile played across her face. It was filled with thanks for all that lay behind her and hope for what might yet be. Franny started her car and drove home, alone.

THE END

BOOKS IN THE SERIES

For updates about new releases, exclusive promotions, and to sign up for the author's mailing list, please visit: www.ahavatrivedi.com/about

ABOUT THE AUTHOR

Ahava Trivedi grew up in the south of England and almost on a whim one day, decided to up and move to Toronto, Canada with her sister.

She is mostly a fiction author who, similar to her hasty move across the pond, likes to explore different genres that interest her by diving headlong into them first and figuring out her story as she goes along.

The author's debut series has taken shape as The Hopeless Husband Series. Stay tuned for other books and series, that are being picked from the ether, plotted and brought into existence as you read these words.

If you'd like to contact Ahava, she'd love to hear from you! Here are some ways to get in touch:

Twitter-verse: @Ahava_T

Facebook Page: Ahava Trivedi Author

Read more at www.ahavatrivedi.com

Printed in Dunstable, United Kingdom